AF268708

SANCTUARY

an experimental anthology of speculative fiction

Compiled by David F. Shultz

Sanctuary: an experimental anthology of speculative fiction
Compiled by David F. Shultz

This is a work of fiction. The stories are products of the author's imagination and are not intended to be construed as real. Any resemblance to actual persons, living or dead, is entirely coincidental.

Published by tdotSpec Inc.
ISBN# 978-1-9994039-2-8

Interior design and cover design by David F. Shultz
Cover illustration by Dominik Gutzeit

Cover Illustration "The Sanctuary" by Dominik Gutzeit / Hydraw-Art
"The Sanctuary" © 2016-2018 Hydraw-Art

ACKNOWLEDGEMENTS

This anthology is the product of an intense, one-day period of writing and editing by a team of writers currently residing in Toronto. It was a joint effort between the *Toronto Science Fiction and Fantasy* writers group and the *Toronto Horror Writers* group. I would like to thank all of the writers for contributing their talent and time in order to make this anthology possible. Thanks, everyone! It was a lot of fun, and we created something awesome, thanks to you!

I would like to thank Myles, "The Itch", who runs the *Toronto Horror Writers* group. Myles helped organize the event, and originally suggested the idea. He also brought along members of his *Toronto Horror Writers* group to add a touch of darkness to the collection. Thanks, Myles, and thanks, horror writers!

And I would also like to thank the reader, whoever you may be, for taking a chance on this very experimental anthology. I hope you enjoy the stories and find the collection interesting. Thanks for reading!

David F. Shultz

INTRODUCTION

We wrote this anthology in one day. Seriously.

It usually takes about a year to produce an anthology. We wondered what would happen if we tried to do it in a day. *Sanctuary* is the result of that experiment.

All of the writers were given the theme "Sanctuary" in advance. They were allowed to come up with ideas, characters, plot elements, or anything else they wanted for planning purposes, based on this theme. But all the writing and editing was done in a single day, most of it over four hours in a marathon writing session at *The Imperial Pub* in downtown Toronto.

We set a firm deadline, and didn't allow any kind of editing to be done after the fact. You're likely to find more spelling and grammatical errors than a typical anthology, more awkward phrasings, and more chaff, which is usually cut during editing.

It's conventional wisdom among experienced writers that most of the work in making a quality product happens during editing and rewrites. I'm sure that's right, but for the sake of this anthology, I hope it isn't *too* right.

We didn't exert any editorial or quality control over the final product. The only requirement was that the stories be legal, with the most likely illegality being copyright infringement. Beyond that, anything that was written by our participating writers made it in.

Some of the writers have included author notes with their contributions to give additional insight into their stories and perspective into the writing process.

Story order is usually something to consider when compiling an anthology. One design consideration is the assignment of so-called "tent-pole" stories to prop up the anthology; an anthology should start with a strong story, end with a strong story, and have a strong story at the mid-point to avoid a "sagging middle". Another consideration is to avoid placing similar stories side-by-side. For a science fiction and fantasy anthology, it's a good idea to alternate between genres, as much as possible. We didn't do any of that here. The stories appear in the order in which they were received.

I was expecting the average length of stories to be around 1 to 1.5 thousand words, which is a professional rate for a good day's work. The average length was 2,130 words. Several writers wrote over 3k words. Two wrote over 5k. One writer completed two stories within the timeframe. The completed anthology includes 21 stories, 1 poem, and 1 screenplay, with a total word count of 49,000 words.

I promise this is not the most polished anthology around. I can almost promise the opposite. But I can also promise that it is interesting. Not just for the imaginative, fun, and diverse stories, which are the product of a large pool of talented writers working feverishly under extreme pressure (and, for some of us, the influence of alcohol), but also as an experiment in literary creation. This is a raw look at what writers can achieve when they set out to create an entire anthology in one day. And, though I may be biased, I think it's awesome.

I hope you have fun reading *Sanctuary*!

David F. Shultz

CONTENTS

NONECISSUS
Emil Pellim

The man and his coworkers arrive at the historic hotel at nine am. The company, oft pressed for finding operational efficiencies, has yet again paid to bus hundreds of people hundreds of kilometers just to announce a new strategy, as if the poor acoustics of a dingy basement conference room will make it more appealing to follow. The man has not said a word to a soul. Moving like mist between bus seats, from coffee station to auditorium, from breakfast platter to bathroom and back. His silence did not begin this early morn. Oh no, it has been so for days. Mute for lack of anything important to say. Should he have to speak today, he would need to crack an egg into a coffee cup and, once sure no shells fell in with the innards, drink it in stringy, gelatinous gulps. That would oil his unused voice box and allow him to make a sound other than a raspy grunt.

But that is not necessary. No one has made an effort to speak to the misty man since sun up. And the boss of the man and of most other people in the hall is clearing his throat loudly which means the scheduled talks will start soon and the silence will be enforced rather than voluntary. The man is perfectly fine with this. He takes a lonesome seat in the very back on the left. He has chosen the spot because there were three empties in a row and that allows him a buffer on both sides. As soon as he touches buttocks to badly padded chair, that other, bigger man, the boss, the one who does have something important to say seemingly all the time, begins to speak.

The news they are all there to receive is that the company is pivoting away from running fleets of self-driving cars in cities one to ten million large, and toward making money from licensing fees of the price optimization algorithms they've developed. It is the third… no, the fourth pivot in as many years. The man looks at the audience and imagines them all collectively as a tiny speck, circling around an enormous whirlpool, getting sucked in. Pivoting about this devouring cyclone seems to be the best they can ever do - circle, circle, circle. They never make progress, never move further away; they are equidistant to doom at all times. Isn't it tiring to spin around the drain for so long? Can't they all just relax their muscles, stop flapping their arms in desperation, and surrender to the currents? Just get it over with and fall into oblivion, instead of eternally pivoting about it.

At the third mention of the proof for something being inside a pudding, the legs of the man take a stand and raise him out of his seat involuntarily. After a hesitant moment he walks off in the direction of the bathroom as a ruse for the onlookers whose attention was attracted by movement between the seats. The man bypasses the bathroom door, however, and keeps walking until he is out into the hotel's courtyard. The waterfront property is mostly quiet. He takes a pack of cigarettes out of his breast pocket and lights one with an almost-empty lighter, flicking three times before the flame survives in the wind long enough to burn the tip of the cigarette. For this particular man, at this particular time, this is not the only task which takes several starts before any headway is made.

The cigarette shrinks slowly. Effort is a hard commodity to come by nowadays for him, even when it comes to taking a drag out of a mood stick. Leaving a trail of smoke behind him, the man walks up to the edge of the water and stares into his reflection. He is framed by the beautiful building behind. His face is not as well-preserved as that of the hotel, even at age thirty-three. There are cracks in the facade, around the eyes and mouth. Lines tracing a permanent scowl. He throws his cigarette at the reflection to burn the image dead, and runs his eyes away from it and across the water to the opposing shore.

There is a moderate forest on the other side, with trees and brush lined up against the edge of the water. The vegetation is reflected on the surface with pristine clarity, every single tree casting an individual image. Reality and reflection in a diptych. But the man's brain spots an error. There is an incongruity between the two, one that he may have missed had it not involved such a particular tree. Directly opposite of him, a large birch stands tall and juts out sideways halfway along its height in a lopsided branch-fork. Its features are coarse and asymmetrical, like the men the man is usually attracted to; busted-sexy. This tree is only present in the part of the image above the water horizon. Its reflection is absent from the natural scene painted on the water's surface.

This absence is inexplicable and certainly warrants closer investigation. The man walks off along the shore to the right, looking for a spot where crossing over would be possible. He's been gone a while. At first he thinks his coworkers will assume he is taking a long shit. Then he mocks himself for thinking his coworkers would even care to consider his whereabouts. Eventually, he comes across an area where the distance between shores narrows into a stream, and he crosses over and ends up with wet and heavy pant legs. Backtracking in the opposite direction, he is united with the jagged tree which keeps its reflection to itself.

He touches the tree half-expecting it to be a birch ghost, but it is solid and real. And so the man turns around and looks at the reflection in the water. He thinks some trick of light will become broken; an optical illusion that obscured the tree when looking from the other side will come to an end. At this time the man lets out an inaudible gasp, almost breaking his silence. Standing there, in the exact spot in front of the birch tree, he is no more visible in the water's mirror than a ghost would be in a non-believer's eyes.

Never has the man been moved quite so. Not by the works at the Dali museum in Figueres. Not by the chiseled rocks of Gobleki Tepe. An entire world revealing itself before him, identical in every way to the one he knows other than a distinct lack of him. The man draws memories of washing his bathroom mirror with glass cleaner and paper towel. Within a day of each wash, a tiny splash of toothpaste thrown loose from the bristles as he brushes would land on the clean mirror and leave a blotch on the surface. Next time he would look at the mirror, that spittle would ruin an otherwise perfect reflection. Not now. The reflection in the water is perfection unruined, the single blemish that is his existence kept at bay by an unknown mechanism.

Casting no sound for days prior, the man casts image neither now. He has not moved since realizing this to be the case. There was consideration of testing this phenomenon, of taking several steps sideways and seeing whether he manifests back into the virtual image on the water. The man even sends distinct commands from his brain to try this. His body does not comply though, as if nerves are severed at the neck, leaving him paralyzed. Maybe out of fear of reappearance; maybe he doesn't want this spell to be broken. Thus the man stands and stares at the beautiful reflection, from pale blue morning until the sky darkens into a dense indigo duvet, gazing through himself into shining stars splashing in the shallow water.

The lights of the hotel across ignite one by one as night smothers day. Motionless, the man hungers and thirsts; he has foregone sustenance in his trance, and he considers again departing from his standing spot. He projects a path to food and drink but his mind shrivels at the thought as if touching an electric fence - food and drink would add to him. They'd weigh him down to the world. So would leaving this place. Food isn't that filling; beer is bitterly delicious but this is better. He remains where his image can only be imagined.

Like sparks spat by fire, the lights of the hotel rooms extinguish as the night progresses. All of the man's co-workers are going to bed. He has missed the remaining talks of the day, he has also missed the social hours after. With a full view of the hotel's yard, he can see that the missing is not mutual - those he works with have not noticed him gone, are not looking for him, are likely not thinking about him; a lot of them would be unable to name him. The man digs his heels further into the soil and stares at his lack of self in the moonlit mirror.

The sun rises and floats on the water, and the man's coworkers rise too, in preparation for exodus by bus back into the city. He is weak, hunger chews at his belly's lining. He sees the busses pull up to the side of the hotel and a chain of humans enter them and start to fill the seats. For the shortest of moments the man desires to be with them, to follow them on their path, to engage on the newest pivot and to paddle against the currents. But his reflection, like his voice, has been gone too long. It's impossible for him to reemerge, and he knows it, so he stops trying and lies down and rests. His disappearance is in the past. Nothing that happens to him from this point on should be mourned further.

BOLT-FOR-BRAINS

Don Miasek

Ms. Chesapeake was talking about the summer break now, and all the safety procedures she expected them to take over the summer holiday. Vinod wasn't listening. Instead he--and all his friends--were staring at the clock on the wall. The time shone in bright green letters, with the seconds slowly counting up.

Tick, tick, tick.

Four minutes to five and the end of class. No more math. No more show-and-tell. No more boring stories about the history of Venus Station Beta. No more kindergarten.

No more flesh and blood, soon. Vinod tried not to think about that. His mom had always told him that these were the best years of his life, and so he should enjoy them. But while his friends were excited for the summer off, Vinod was scared.

Tick, tick, tick.

Something nudged Vinod in his back. He squirmed around in his seat to look behind him. Charles held a note out for him, and Vinod unraveled it.

Calvball? it said.

Vinod nodded enthusiastically and handed the note back. One last game of Calvball, and he'd be separated from his friends forever.

A loud buzzing rang throughout the classroom, and Vinod jolted in his seat. In his thoughts, the four minutes had passed.

"Alright now," Ms. Chesapeake called out over the noise of everyone packing up their bags and gadgets, "Everyone have a good time off. Remember, 'a careful student is a safe student'."

Vinod lined up with the fifty other kids as they filed out of the room. The doors were flanked by two soldiers with big guns and big armor.

"Have a good time, kids," one of the soldiers said as they passed by. "Have a safe time."

The other soldier said nothing. He was focused on running a scanner over each of them. Anyone and anything could be an explosive, mom always said. Vinod had never seen it in person, but the newsfeeds on VenusNet were proof of that. Once mom let him watch a vid of a school levelled by an explosion. Instead of a shining building, there was only broken metal and rubble.

He'd cried all night, even though mom said he'd never have to worry about that. But she also said he wasn't allowed to watch the vids anymore.

Vinod stood shoulder to shoulder with the others, hoping nobody noticed him secretly standing on his toes. It made him look like a big kid, and if he was a big kid he wouldn't be picked last for teams. Nobody wanted to be picked last for Calvball.

"Um, we'll take Amy," said Jake.

Amy bounced out of the line and lined up with Jake's team. There were only four left of the unchosen players.

Whoever got picked last was the biggest loser, Vinod knew, and he looked over at the others in the line. Charles whispered into the other Team Captain's ear. Vinod hoped Charles was telling

Madra to pick him. Madra nodded, but then pointed at someone else. "I'll take Robart."

Vinod could feel the tears welling up in his eyes. That wasn't fair! Robart was fat and missed even the easiest catches. I'm a way better player than Robart! he thought. Yet it was Robart who happily joined Madra's team.

Three left.

Vinod wondered if Charles really told Madra to pick him or not. Maybe Madra had just ignored Charles. Charles was his friend, and he wouldn't just leave him to be the biggest loser. Yet something in Vinod's mind made him wonder.

"Rebecca," Jake said without hesitation.

Two left. Just him and the dummy Eldren, who looked over at him. Vinod knew what Eldren was thinking, because he was thinking the same thing. If you aren't picked last, then you aren't the biggest loser. Nobody wanted that.

I'm faster! Vinod wanted to shout. I can jump and I can catch, and I can throw better than half the kids in the school yard, even if I was only in kindergarten. But he knew shouting that would just get him in trouble. Soldiers lined the Calvball field, and he knew they wouldn't hesitate to run over if someone caused trouble.

Charles leaned over into Madra's ear and whispered again. Please be telling her to pick me! Vinod thought. Madra shrugged back at Charles and then pointed. "I guess I'll take Eldren."

"No!" Vinod shouted, but he knew it was stupid the moment he did it. "That isn't fair!"

"Ha ha, loser bolt-for-brains got picked last!" Jake crowed. He was way bigger than everyone else. Jake was in the second grade.

Vinod felt his face turning red. "I am NOT bolt-for-brains!" he shouted.

"You will be soon," Jake taunted. "They're gonna scoop out your brains." He made a gross noise with his mouth. "Shllluuurpp!"

"No they won't!" Vinod ran up to him.

"Oh my God, bolt-for-brains doesn't even know what happens during augmentation."

"Stop calling me that!" Vinod knew he was crying but couldn't stop the tears from flowing.

"You're gonna be a machiiiine!" Jake sang. "You're gonna be a machiiiiine!" He looked at the others, and they slowly joined in. Nobody wanted to get on the bad side of a second grader.

Vinod was aghast. This was his worst nightmare come to life. He wished he could just wake up and do this day again. Then he'd say no to Charles and not even go out for stupid Calvball. He looked over at Charles, and to his horror his friend had joined in with the singing.

"Charrrrles!" Vinod cried.

Charles stopped singing. He looked embarrassed, but Vinod knew that was because he was known to be his friend. "Sorry Vinod, but you aren't gonna be 'round no more. We aren't gonna be able to hang out once they scoop your brains."

"You're my friend!" Tears were running down Vinod's cheeks. He wiped them off, but he knew everyone had already seen. Now he was the biggest loser AND a crybaby.

"Boop, boop, bolt-for-brains Vinod is having his last emotion!" Jake laughed. "Shlrrrrp!" The others made the noise too.

"Ms. Chesapeake has cybernetics and she isn't a bolt-for-brains!"

"That's different." Jake gave that big sigh that adults gave when they were trying to explain things to little kids, but Vinod wasn't a little kid no more. He was out of kindergarten. "Ms. Chesapeake just has a little cybernetics. My dad says that's completely normal. What you're gonna get be is a full-convert. You're gonna be a bolt-for-brains hooked up to a computer, and we're never gonna have to see you again."

Vinod looked over at the soldiers lining the Calvball field. They must have heard the shouting by now. Why didn't they come over and tell Jake to stupid being such a jerk? Vinod wished they would.

In all the VR flicks Vinod had seen, this was where the plucky young kid would punch the bully's lights out, even though the bully was thirty centimeters taller. Bam! Pow! The bully would go down and all the kids would cheer, and everything would be alright from then on.

Mom always said those VR flicks were stupid and weren't real. Vinod knew that--he didn't need an adult telling him--but part of him hoped that maybe in this case it just might be true. Stories were built on the kernel of truth, according to Ms. Chesapeake.

Vinod brought his fist around and smooshed it against Jake's chest as hard as he could. For a moment, the bigger kid looked stunned, and Vinod hoped it was because he'd been knocked right out. But then Jake laughed and shoved him back.

Vinod stumbled and fell onto his butt, dirt spraying everywhere.

"Bolt-for-brains, bolt-for-brains!" Jake shouted. The bigger kid was on him in a second, and all Vinod could feel was the rain of fists crashing against his face. "Bolt-for-brains, bolt-for-brains!"

What happened next Vinod could only barely remember. Jake pummeled him like only a bigger kid should. He heard the others shouting, and through the haze of pain he wondered why Charles wasn't helping him. Nobody could be friends with a bolt-for-brains crybaby who was the biggest loser.

"Knock it off!" someone shouted. It was an adult voice. In a moment, Jake was hoisted off of him and into the arms of one of the soldiers.

Vinod wished the soldiers had stopped them before he'd ever been picked last.

"You goddamn kids!" the soldier shouted into Jake's face. She was right furious now, and Vinod hoped she'd punch Jake's lights out. But instead the soldier only spoke. "We're trying to protect you from terrorists and you stupid children are pulling this kind of shit!?"

Now Jake was crying, even as the soldier set him back down. Good, Vinod thought. Let him have a taste of his own medicine.

"Your parents'll be hearing about this," the soldier said, though Vinod thought she sounded a bit worried. Soldiers weren't supposed to touch the kids, even if it was to break up a fight. They definitely weren't supposed to swear at them, neither.

Charles stood over Vinod and held out a hand.

But Vinod was in no mood to take it. That would be forgiving stupid Charles, and Vinod couldn't give him the satisfaction. He climbed back to his feet on his own. He wished he could stand tall. The kids in the VR flicks would say something clever and make the bully cry even more, but Vinod was no VR flick kid.

"H-h-he punched me!" Vinod bawled instead, pointing at Jake. "He called me a bolt-for-brains and he punched me!"

"Oh for Christ's sake," the soldier muttered. "You're going to be one of those full-convert deals."

That nearly stunned Vinod out of crying. A second grader saying that being a bolt-for-brains was bad was one thing, but an adult? He'd never be able to show his face in public again.

Vinod didn't look at any of the other kids, but he hoped they felt bad about the way he'd been treated. He'd been their friend ever since pre-school. He wished he could tell them all off, but instead he just grabbed his Calvball gloves and knapsack and ran off the field.

"Hey, kid," the soldier called out. "Don't just run away." But she did nothing to actually stop him.

Vinod ran all the way to the vacuum train terminal. Along the way, he wiped the snot off his face as best he could with his sleeve, but one look at his reflection in the station's chrome walls still showed puffy cheeks and red eyes. Everyone else on the train would know he was a big crybaby. With his Calvball gloves, he bet all the adults knew he'd been picked last.

The trip home was a half-hour by vacuum train. Vinod kept looking at his phone, hoping there'd be some message from the other kids. They'd be all apologizing for the way they acted, and saying that Jake was actually the biggest loser and how they never should have sung bolt-for-brains at him. But there were no messages from anyone. All of them had abandoned him, and Vinod felt that his eyes were as big as discs now. He hoped none of the adult passengers on the train saw it.

The train dropped him off in front of his building. It was the biggest on Venus Beta, and Ms. Chesapeake always said the VenusNet Data Center was the most important of all. None of the other kids seemed to see it that way, though.

Vinod stopped and waited at the security station for the man to signal him through. Soon he was running for the door at the end of the long dark hallway. It chimed as he approached, sliding open. The lights flickered on as he stepped in.

"Moo-oom!" he cried as he entered the apartment and threw down his gloves and knapsack. Big kids weren't supposed to cry for their moms, but Vinod didn't care. Jake and Charles and Eldren and the soldiers weren't there to see him anymore.

He found her in her work alcove, which is where she normally was at this time of day. Her arms and legs looked like a skeleton's as she laid in her bed under the protective glass of her capsule. A silvery sheet was all that covered her otherwise naked body. Thick cables, colored in each ribbon of the rainbow, ran from the chrome plating in her head and the computer banks lining the walls and ceiling. Her eyes were shut, but Vinod knew she could still see him through all the cameras around the room.

"Mom, Charles and Jake punched me!"

Mom did not answer.

"MOM!" he shouted again, and this time she stirred.

The huge machinery hooked up above her head whirred and ka-chunked. Her eyes suddenly fluttered open, and she smiled as she saw who was standing above her. "Oh my dear sweet Vinod. How was your last day at school?" Her voice came through the computer system.

"I hated it," Vinod bawled, and it all tumbled out. He told her about being picked last at Calvball, how Jake was mean to him, and how Charles didn't do anything to help. He didn't mention trying to punch Jake, or how the soldier had to break up the fight.

Mom listened to every word, but Vinod suspected she didn't truly understand just how bad of a day it was. "Oh Vinod, I'm so sorry."

"Can you tell Jake's mom what he did?" Vinod hoped Jake would get spanked--she was a known authoritarian.

That made mom hesitate, but then she gave the slightest shake of her head. "I-- no, no. We'd best not trouble Jake's mother. In a little while you won't have to worry about any of that. None of your friends will matter, soon enough. You're going to be augmented, soon."

Vinod bit his lower lip. Even if he hated Jake and Charles and Rebecca and all the others, he didn't know if he wanted to never see them again.

"Full-convert cyborg means safety, Vinod. It means protection," mom said softly. "Once you're part of VenusNet, no-one can ever hurt you."

For some reason, that didn't make Vinod any less scared. "But mom," he sniffled.

"No buts, Vinod. Jake and Charles and all the others will envy you after augmentation. No name-calling and no bullies."

Vinod couldn't help but like the sound of that, even if it meant they wouldn't be his friends anymore.

"There are bad men and women out there," mom went on. "There are terrorists, and criminals, and mean people who would hurt you all throughout Venus Beta. I will never lose you the way we did your father. Do you understand?"

Vinod nodded, but still sniffled.

"Do you want a hug?"

Vinod nodded. It wasn't every day he got a hug.

Mom smiled, and her fingers twitched as the command was sent through the network.

SANITATION PROCEDURES STARTED a computerized voice said. Gases shot through mom's capsule, and she gasped as she gulped down the clean air.

Vinod fidgeted with his hands as he waited, wondering what his own capsule would look like.

SANITATION PROCEDURES COMPLETED

Mom's capsule creaked as the glass jolted up into the ceiling, exposing her to the apartment air. Her cracked lips tugged upwards in a motherly smile, and she held her gangly arms out for him. Vinod gladly climbed into them and hugged her back with all his might.

"My dear, sweet Vinod," she said. "No-one can ever hurt us in here."

Author's Note

I'd say I got done pretty much everything I wanted to with this story. If I had more time then it would probably be spent fleshing out Vinod's mother and what her deal is. But, that's the nature of doing everything in one afternoon.

Writing from the perspective of a five or six year old was a lot of fun. I've learned that nobody on Earth can agree on what narrative should sound like coming from a child.

ORANGE RIVERS

Sasha R

Cowards warned us of green fires
Biting rain and nature's ire
Rotting lungs and blistering sockets
Of the oceans surging black

Yet we had no fear of vengeance
Metal beasts kept to their rampage
Through the glistening seas and jungles
Crushing all that won't submit

Still the day came when the fallen
Rose to bite the light that scorched them
Waves gashed roaring through our fortress
Hungry winds tore at our skin

As we climbed the trembling mountains
Hiding, crawling, weeping, brawling
Praying for the gods and angels
Take our plight and set us free

Only one has shown us mercy
Lead us surely, smiling softly

To belong brave, bright and burning
In his halls within the deep

We gave up our flesh and sorrows
To the demons in his burrow
Singing of eternal fire
To the innards of the earth

Shining true among the shadows
Free in boiling, orange rivers
Dancing frenzied with the devil
Shrieking glory to his flames

Here the wild's rage won't harm us
Here no shame or tears will plague us
Here we'll rule in silky darkness
Till the world is only ash

FLORA

K.M.

People leave things all the time.

As a bartender I had seen it all—wallets, earrings, and even a coat in the deep of winter. How someone did not miss that boggled me.

The bottle sitting on the counter didn't draw my attention. Walk by it one way, and then the next, and the next after that, until it was closing, and it was still there.

My instinct? Throw it out.

I picked it up, raised a brow. It looked old. Wood, carved and polished. The type you see in the homes of shamans and voodoo people. I wasn't exactly intrigued, but disgusted that I'd picked it up.

"Whatchu got there?" Barrie asked, breathing over my shoulders.

I exhaled. "I have no idea. A water bottle?"

Barrie scowled. "Looks strange."

"Yeah," I said, allowing my eyes to gleam over the squiggly symbols, barely visible on its squat, four inch tall body. Calling it a water bottle was a stretch, but I didn't know what it was. "Someone left it here, I guess."

"Well, it doesn't look important, so you know what to do with it." He walked off, disappearing into the backroom.

I knew what to do with it—dump it.

It was closing time. I'd done two shifts worth of work today, and my feet burned. I was all ready to collapse into my unmade bed in the north end of the city.

The bin was overstuffed, spilling over its top, because people just don't get the separation of waste rule—compost, organic, plastic, glass, yada. The next nearest bin was too far across the room, and even from here, I saw the same mass-pileup problem. I pushed the bottle into the bin, squashing empty food cartons and cans further down. A second after I walked away, a pile of rubbish spilled out onto the floor. A clang. The bottle rolled toward me.

Damn. Now I had to clean up.

Barrie stuck his big head out from the backroom. "You okay over there, Sammie?"

"Ah, yeah," I said, and sighed.

Cleaning up was slow. Soon I was hauling the overstuffed garbage bags, wondering why Barrie couldn't order a bigger bin. I was a scrawny woman, barely over a hundred pounds, and my muscles weren't trained for this. The bottle was the last thing I reached for, and I grabbed it and hissed when its metal clasp lid came undone. I barely got time to react before a green powdery gas seeped out from the container and doused me and the space around me. I covered my eyes and groaned. That was an instinct thing. I coughed, inhaling some greenish, herbal smelling stuff that burned my throat and nostrils.

"Ah choo!" My lungs clogged up and so did my sinuses. When I wandered from the bar some thirty minutes later, the bottle safely in the bin, and not a second thought given to it, I was feeling alright, not sick.

That night, I had the most bizarre fever dream. I was standing in a place covered in glowing green plants and moss. The critters were loud in my ears. And then I woke to my phone ringing. I grabbed it on maybe the third or fourth ring, while still lying in bed.

"Yeah?"

"You need to get to the bar, like right now." Click. Barrie hung up.

I stared at the phone and then the alarm clock. Shit. I jumped from bed and stumbled to the washroom. It was past four in the evening. I slept through the start of my shift.

In the bathroom, I changed only my underwear and washed my face, not even glancing to it, before I was out the door, wishing Barrie wouldn't fire me like he'd done all the other employees. I had a massive credit card debt to pay off. How could I have overslept?

Ah- choo!

Shit, was I coming down sick?

The door to the bar was locked, and I spent a solid half a minute trying to pry it open before I remembered that we weren't officially opened yet, and so I moved to the side door. It was pushing six when I got in. I noticed the odor first. Aromatic. Did Barrie spray the place with air freshener? My nose guided me into the main bar, and I stopped in my tracks, gasping, eyes scanning the room in wonder. Had I stepped into a jungle?

Maybe I entered the wrong place, not the swarmy cheap little pub with the bad food where I'd been working for two years. I turned on my heels, heading back to the door, when Barrie called my name.

Wide-eyed, I faced him. Middle-aged, scruffy, and not exactly sharply dressed in oversized T-shirt and khaki pants, he stepped closer to me, looking unalarmed. What the heck was going on? What had he done to the bar?

"This happened overnight," he said calmly, hands sweeping the room.

"I don't understand. How?" My eyes swept the bar, glowing moss-covered walls, vines, one of which swung from one end of the wall to the next, blending back into the vegetation, as if it was a living being.

"I don't know. I was hoping you would know."

My brows creased. "Are you serious?"

"You were last here."

"We left together."

He sighed. "I was gonna call the authorities, but this isn't a fire, or a robbery." His eyes swept the room, landing on the counter, a shrine of green shrubbery and leaves, all glowing. "What do you think caused this?"

I shrugged. And then I remembered something—my dream. The jungle. The glowing plants. And before that, the bottle, spilling open with the green powder. "That bottle. There was some powder in it."

Barrie's brows arched. "A powder caused this?"

I shrugged. "What are we gonna do?"

"I tried ripping the things off the wall, but they just grow back into place. Even tried setting fire. They're resistant. I have my own rainforest here."

"Why so calm about this?"

Barrie eyed me. "There's something else you gotta see."

He walked off and I tailed him, to behind the counter, the door that led into our kitchen and storage. He glanced at me before turning the lock. A flood of shine and glare hit me. The plants, blue, green, purple, bioluminescent. I shielded my eyes. "It leads to *some* place." His words were lost on me at first but then I realized we weren't standing in the kitchen anymore. This *some place* he spoke of was a lush forest, alive with the music of critters. Where our sink used to be, I spotted the small glowing creatures, big-eyed and salamander-like, slithering around. "They came with the place."

Our eyes met. "What are you thinking?"

"Whatever was in that bottle was an entire ecosystem." He paused and his eyes were lost in some distant thought. "If the authorities come, they'll shut us down. Maybe we can see about this first."

"See about…?" Ah-choo!

"You alright?"

There was green-stained blood on my fingers that had come from my nose. It sparkled. Shit. I faced him. "I ingested some of the green powder."

Barrie's eyes narrowed down on me. "You need a hospital?"

I shook my head, a little feverish. Maybe that wasn't a bad idea to see a doctor. I trembled, and wilted, and then my vision blurred.

Next I woke in a hospital, and Barrie was there, speaking softly to me. "You're gonna be fine," he told me, and then proceeded, in the same soft tone, to explain that he planned on keeping the bar situation on the down low. I didn't understand why he would. But days later, after I'd gotten out of the hospital, my fever settled, I returned to the bar. Barrie walked from the kitchen area. He looked up, happy.

"It's still the same," I said. The moss and bioluminescent plants had thickened, and now carpeted the floor. I didn't feel comfortable, not with the look of the place, and not with my own body. The doctors had said I was alright, but there were things that haunted me. I slept and dreamed of greenery, and seeing what was supposed to be the bar now, I could hear the sounds of the critters, swarming my ears. Barrie extended a finger to one of the glowing, bug-eyed salamander creatures from the kitchen that leaped onto his right shoulder, demonstrating a disturbing ease. "They've been asking for you."

My eyes found his, half a foot above mine. "What do you mean?"

He exhaled, hands on his hips. "It seems you are chosen like me."

"I don't get it."

"While you were away, I had gotten to the bottom of why a flora has taken over my bar. As it turns out, they're visitors from another world. Everything they were was in that bottle. They're seeking a new home."

The revelation was sickening, but I'd already known. My dreams.

Barrie chuckled. "They can speak you know." His eyes washed over the walls with the crawling vegetation. "Try speaking to them. They want to hear from you." Barrie yanked my hand and dragged me to the wall.

I pulled away. "Why are you okay with this?"

He glanced at me, not understanding at first, and then he sighed. "I didn't have the heart to tell you, but we're going under. We're done. A few weeks more."

"You would've let me find out through a notice on the door."

He shrugged. "But this is gonna be our saving grace."

"How?"

"Think of it —tourism."

My eyes were daggers stabbing into him. "You can't be serious."

"I am."

"And how will you control this?"

His eyes narrowed on me. "They're reasonable. They just need our help."

Alarmed, I shook my head and stormed out, thinking he was mad. The jungle stayed on my mind. Barrie's mind couldn't change. He was convinced the vegetation that took over the bar could be controlled. It couldn't. When I next returned to the bar, driven by a fever and a desire to be there, haunted by vision, and the determination to drag him to safety, I saw the extent of the madness. There was almost no place to walk. Moss carpeted the floor, the counter transformed into shrub.

"Barrie!"

No answer, no matter how loudly I bellowed his name.

Last night I'd dreamed that the vegetation strangled him.

When I finally faced the wall with the glowing moss and slithering vines, its echoes drummed into my head. It had a heart, a life force, and it throbbed, calling out to me, luring me. Before I put my hand on it, shuffling alerted me to the bar counter.

I spun, finding Barrie standing wobbly with a look of dishevelment. Beads of sweat broke out across his face, and he looked gaunter than I'd seen him days earlier. He'd also been wearing the same clothes.

"Barrie," I said and marched over.

He glanced towards me, distressed. "They're coming—all of them, the colony."

"What?"

"Went over. Deeper, further. They're coming. It's not good."

I swallowed. "I know. Barrie we have to get out of here and call the authorities."

"Too late," he said, and then collapsed.

I threw myself down next to this body, shaking him. He was on fire, sweating, and barely breathing. A second later, vines ripped off the wall, one after the other, and leashed him. Stunned, I watched as they dragged him toward the wall, glowing bright green and misted up. "Barrie!" I shouted. He was gone, vanishing into the moss-covered wall.

Shit!

I spun, eyes washing over my surroundings. The vegetation was noisy. Shifting, slithering plants, all at once closing in. Eyes on the exit, breath in my throat, I pushed forward, but the door was covered by glowing greenery. A leafy vine leashed my neck, strangling me, stifling my scream. I struggled with the vines, failing, as one after the other roped me until I was coiled in plants.

Barrie's voice. A vessel. The thing I'd seen in the vision last night that made me return here. Alien, a colony of intelligent vegetation that swarmed and overrun sapient beings. Those critters living in it, they weren't insects but sapient beings, people like me, absorbed by it. Whoever had left this bottle behind fucked us.

This was colonization 101. The vegetation was melding itself with my skin. I was on fire, as my entire being got sucked in, blending with it, until we were the same. From the corner of my eyes, I saw Barrie, sculpted into the moss of the chittering walls. They were speaking. The last words I heard before I succumbed.

A new home.

THE GADGET IS IN THE SAFE PLACE

K. Connor

EXT LOW RISE OFFICE BUILDING - NIGHT

A large barely lit parking lot is scattered with a few cars. A lone SECURITY GUARD slowly walks the perimeter.

INT LAB - NIGHT

The lights are off. Computers jam what should be a spacious lab. A seemingly empty room vibrates from the hum of running code. Monitors exude a gloomy glow emoting an eerie feel.

INT LAB DESK - NIGHT

TRISHA (an Archie Panjabi type), stares at the reams of code that surround her. She yawns and palms Chinese stress balls around and around.

CRASH!

Trisha's stress balls stop moving.

She looks behind her into the dark but sees nothing.

Her desktop monitor fades up to reveal a friendly human face. MANNY (an Idris Elba look alike) is scowling on the Telecom Video Phone App in front of her.

                    MANNY
          Did you hear that?

Trisha swallows hard and grabs her cell phone. She taps the light on and waves it white flag style toward the back of the room.

A CAT darts from under the mess.

                    TRISHA
          It's that rang a tang cat from the other
          office.

                    MANNY
          Take care of it will ya? We don't need
          security snooping around.

                    TRISHA
          That security guy is basically a Keystone
          Cop. Relax. No one out there will find out
          what is happening in these 4 walls, I
          guarantee you.

                    MANNY

This is rolling the dice of disaster in my opinion.

Suddenly, a Security Guard knocks on the window as flashlight beams shine through.

Trisha jumps up and waves the Guard away.

The Guard waves back and saunters into the dark of the dimly lit parking lot.

Trisha fumbles unsuccessfully with the blinds for more privacy.

> TRISHA
>
> Really.. Can you just let it be? It's fine. If you would just stop distracting me, we could complete the Gadget testing with calm precision.

> MANNY
>
> I've been running codes 24/7 for months now. I don't need your over confident ego getting in the way of the end goal. K?

> TRISHA
>
> Your point?

> MANNY
>
> The Gadget will not be welcome by all the powers that be. We know this. We need to be cautious.

> TRISHA
> All inventions disrupt the order of things.
> Again, you are over thinking it. The Gadget
> will save lives. We will be heros. Don't
> punk out on me now!

A shadow comes over Trisha and her work desk. She spins around ready for fight or flight.

A THIEF (a dead ringer for Jada Pinkett Smith) grabs her by the throat. Hard.

They fight and are evenly matched.. Until, they are not.

Trisha wins out.

Manny has watched the entire sequence with some concern from the Telecom Video.

> MANNY (O.S.)
> What'll you do with her?

> TRISHA
> Same thing I did with the last one.

> CUT TO:

INT. LAB STORAGE CLOSET - NIGHT

Trisha manages a complicated lock system and flings the doors open.

She drags the Thief by the legs and pulls her deep into the darkness. She props her up against a back wall and taps her phone light on.

She stands over her captive.

A badly beaten OLD MAN (must be a twin of William Shatner) is propped up close by.

OLD MAN
Hey.

TRISHA

Hey yourself.

OLD MAN
Caught another one I see.

TRISHA

Yup.

OLD MAN
She looks like trouble.

TRISHA

I think you're right.

OLD MAN

Look, I'll say it again. I'm not here to steal anything. Obviously. I just want to talk.

                    TRISHA

I'm not selling you my Gadget. I said No.

                    OLD MAN

Look, someone will either buy it for exploitation or steal it for exploitation. Either way, I'm the lesser of two evils. Embrace it.

                    TRISHA

I disagree. I don't have to choose between two evils. I can do things my own way and slide right up the middle. Get it?

                    OLD MAN

The world doesn't work that way honey. You're overstepping.

Trisha flashes a cheeky smile.

                    TRISHA

If you'd excuse me, I need to run one final test.

EXT LAB STORAGE CLOSET DOORS - NIGHT

Trisha locks up. She hears Manny calling her from across the lab.

INT LAB DESK - NIGHT

Manny waits on the Telecom Video as Trisha collapses into her
chair.

                    MANNY
          Took you long enough.

                    TRISHA
          The Old Guy was yamming on.

                    MANNY
          And the other?

                    TRISHA
          Still out cold. Basically.

The intercom BUZZES loud. Trisha bolts toward it.

                    MANNY (O.S.)
          What the hell?

                    TRISHA
          It's the intercom!

Trisha is careful. She presses the talk button.

                    TRISHA
          Can I help you?

                    WOMAN

I think I have your stuff.

TRISHA
Oh. Yes. I'll come down.

WOMAN
Wait. I'd rather you just buzz me in. OK?
There is a Security Guard creeping around
out here.

Trisha considers.

She buzzes the Woman in. Runs back to her desk, grabs money
from her purse, and waits closely back by the door.

She waits for what seems like forever.

Finally, there is small KNOCKING. Trisha opens it.

The Woman (a dead ringer for Megan Fox) forces herself in.

WOMAN
You have some nosy security out there!

TRISHA
Do you have it?

WOMAN
Pay me first?

Trisha gives her the cash. The Woman gives her a bag.

The Woman stands there. Unmoving.

TRISHA

You can go now.

WOMAN

I don't think I should.

TRISHA

Why not?

WOMAN

Cause the Security detail you got out there,
is tough to slip.

Trisha smirks.

TRISHA

You mean the Keystone Cop?

MANNY (O.S.)

Here we go..

WOMAN

Who is that?

The Woman moves toward where Manny holds court.

MANNY

Let me see you.

The Woman slides into Trisha's chair.

> MANNY
> And you are?

> WOMAN
> The drug dealer.

> MANNY
> Of course you are.

Trisha leans in behind the Woman, and scowls at Manny.

> TRISHA
> Relax will you? I did what I had to, to test
> my Gadget one last time.

> MANNY
> This is a bad idea.

> WOMAN
> Oxy is never a bad idea, my friend.

KNOCK. KNOCK. KNOCK.

All three hit the deck!

It's the Security Guard again. Knocking incessantly on the window, beaming a flashlight through the blinds.

Trisha moves quickly to wave the Guard away.

The Guard waves and once again, saunters back into the darkness.

Trisha fiddles with the blinds to close them but leaves them all tangled.

The Woman goes back to first position and Manny fades up back on the desktop. Both sigh in relief.

INT LAB - STEEL DOOR - NIGHT

Trisha walks to a large steel door. The kind you see in restaurant kitchens. For such a small lab, there's a lot of storage spaces with lots of doors.

She punches in a code and cranks the handle down to open.

Inside, is a testing facility surrounded by shelves of pharmaceutical drugs. Trisha walks to a steel table.

The Woman waits at the entry.

                    WOMAN
          Do you mind?

Trisha hesitates and then nods, allowing the Woman to come in too.

                    TRISHA
          Who are you going to tell.

The Woman trails Trisha inside and looks around.

Trisha dumps the bag of OXY out on the table.

She keys in some computer passwords on the adjacent keyboard and walks to the back room to a steel locked case.

She unlocks it and take out THE GADGET. It is impressive and expensive looking but still kind of resembles a scanner at a grocery store.

Suddenly, we hear muffled YELLING.

                    WOMAN
          Whose that?

                    TRISHA
          Oh. I forgot about them. Bad people.
          They're in a safe place, don't worry.

The Woman is okay with that.

                    WOMAN
          A sanctuary for bad people. How original.

The Woman grins. She looks so clever.

Trisha uses The Gadget to scan the Oxy.

The Gadget has a small monitor on it that shows the percentage make up of various elements in the Oxy.

Trisha uploads the results to the Computer beside her.

The Computer prints out a page of results.

Trisha grabs it and shows the Woman.

> WOMAN
>
> Is that what I think it is?

> TRISHA
>
> Yup.

> WOMAN
>
> Wow. Better than a breathalyzer.

Trisha points to a line on the print out.

> TRISHA
>
> Recognize that?

> WOMAN
>
> Says my Oxy has Fentanyl in it.

> TRISHA
>
> Ya. You are a very bad bitch.

They stand there looking at each other for a moment.

Then the Woman lunges at Trisha.

Trisha turns the Gadget upside around and TASERS the shit out of her.

The Woman drops to the ground and quivers on the floor

> TRISHA

Oh, my bad.

Trisha drags The Woman by the legs to the storage closet.

Manny is yelling on the Telecom Video in the background.

> MANNY (O.S.)
I can hear you dragging her!

> TRISHA
Treasures come to the brave Buddy. I'm taking her to the safe place..for bad people.

Trisha giggles. Manny sighs.

INT LAB STORAGE CLOSET - NIGHT

Trisha pulls the Woman inside and props her up beside the others.

> TRISHA
Three for three. I'm invincible.

Trisha walks out of the storage closet and locks up.

As she turns to get back to Manny, she BUMPS smack into the Security Guard (who looks strangely like Jamie Lee Curtis).

> SECURITY GUARD
Hi.

                    TRISHA
Hello there, Officer.

                 SECURITY GUARD
I'm not an Officer.

                    TRISHA
Oh. Right. You are the Security Guard I
hired.

                 SECURITY GUARD
Yes. That's me.

                    TRISHA
OK. Well, all is well...here..so, you don't
need to worry about a thing.

                 SECURITY GUARD
You seem to have a few problems
in....there.

                    TRISHA
Nothing I can't handle.

Beat.

                 TRISHA (CONT'D)
Why don't you go circle the parking lot.
Check the perimeter. And ..I'll call the
cops. Sound good?

SECURITY GUARD
That won't be necessary.

TRISHA
Why not?

SECURITY GUARD
I'm looking for Sanctuary.

Trisha looks at the lab storage closet warily.

The Security Guard grins.

Somehow she has gotten a hold of the Gadget.

She dials up the TASER function to HIGH. And closes in on Trisha.

On Trisha's shocked face..

MANNY (O.S.)
Is that the Keystone Cop? .....Trish?....

ZAP! ZAP! ZAP!

As Trisha moans, we..

FADE TO BLACK...

PRETA

Jayant Avva

A philosopher of some renown once said that people never ask plaintive questions of God when things are going well. They only ask them when things go wrong. I was no different. When I got through graduate school with good grades, the question "God, why me?" didn't really show up in my mind. When I got a well paying job after graduating, I didn't ask that question either. When I had an amazing relationship with a woman who appeared perfect for me, the question didn't make its appearance. The refrain in my mind in such circumstances was "More, please!"

That question showed up swiftly, seemingly unbidden, when I lost that well paying job. It also showed up when that "perfect woman" decided she fancied another lad. It showed up last week, once more, when I heard that a cancer has metastasized in my brain, as though a tiny machine gun loaded with cancerous tissue had gone off in my head.

"God, why me?!"

Six months. Maybe. Doctors who speak to terminal patients usually throw in all manner of caveats and cautions and express all manner of doubt. Maybe my doctor was terribly concerned with being sued. Or maybe she didn't want to raise my hopes. I could have given a rat's ass at that point.

No answers were forthcoming. Karma? Maybe, but an explanation was small comfort to my mind. When my mind is in a bad place, I usually take long walks in and around Riverdale Park. Tonight, like all nights since my diagnosis, I walked up the familiar dirt road that led into park off of Broadview Avenue.

There is a curious state of mental affairs, where your thoughts are so tortured that you decide to avoid them whenever they show up, by directing your attention elsewhere. I did that just then, and paid attention to the park as I'd never before.

It was late, and it was a moonless night. The park was illuminated solely by the trickle of ambient light off the streets that bounded it, and by a cluster of lights that lit up a large statue of Sun Yat Sen in the park. The sound of crickets became louder as I moved into the darker areas of the park.

Riverdale Park has a steep incline on one side, which spans four or five stories. This leads from Broadview Avenue down into the park. I was at the elevated end of the park. I noticed something shining right in the center of that incline. It was as though someone had placed something like a floodlight there, in the grass that formed the incline. Yet it didn't throw light outward. Its light was confined to narrow cone around the light source.

I walked down the incline, approaching the mysterious light source at the center of the incline from its right. The light source had a blinding center. I've heard of the 'light at the end of the tunnel' experience when you're actively dying. I wondered whether this was some sort of massive trick that my mind was playing, as I lay dying on the grass elsewhere in the park.

Nope. Don't go there. Tonight - no thoughts of cancer!

I attended to the brilliant light that was few feet from me. I couldn't really make out what it was. At one point the grass ended and the cone of peripheral light started. Just a few inches within the periphery, the light became floodlight level, and stayed that way.

Impending death brings with it a certain recklessness. What did I have to lose? A few months of a diseased life? I reached out and touched the periphery of the light. It felt warm, but quite pleasantly so. I went right ahead and plunged my right hand into the brightness. I expected heat but it felt cool instead.

My body felt an enormous energy pulling it towards the light. My entire body felt cooler, even though I had been perspiring a minute before from heat and humidity. I felt bathed in that same coolness, but I couldn't see anything. I was surrounded by white. I lost consciousness after a short while.

I opened my eyes after some length of time. I felt incredibly free. I felt as though my whole body was healed. No more metastatic cancer. I stood up, but found myself lighter than I remembered. Then I saw them.

There were thousands of them, or perhaps millions. The human brain loses the capacity for calculation when the numbers get really high. They glowed like numberless light bugs. They hovered around in clusters, a thousand in a cluster on my right, another hundred in a cluster on my left. They had tiny mouths and large bellies, and they looked all too human.

"He can see us," one of them whispered.

I looked around. I was no longer in Riverdale Park. I saw what appeared to be the wall of a cave behind me, with many of these 'creatures' in front. Perhaps I was in an enormous cave whose distant boundaries were lost in the darkness.

A cluster of them approached me, and I felt an enormous craving for spicy food. The craving became stronger as they drew closer to me. As they surrounded me, I felt this raw existential hunger, as though I would die if I did not consume a tiny spicy treat. One of them looked into my eyes. She was older than me, and her cheeks were sallow and shrunken, and her eyes had retreated deep within her eye sockets. I felt myself gasp noiselessly. Within those barely visible eyes was the same enormous craving that I felt in my belly.

She hovered closer to me, naked as the day she was born. Her pale teats were shrunken and diseased, covered with pus-emitting boils. Below that she sported a swollen belly. Her grotesqueness did nothing to dampen the enormous craving for spicy food in my system. She leaned forward, as though she meant to kiss me. I started and leaned back, but she was upon me. I felt her fangs touch my skin, and I felt her disappointment when they didn't break the surface. Was I not fit for consumption by a ghoulish entity? Was my diseased body not worthy of even that last utility?

She shook her head, and her eyes resumed the same hungry look that I'd seen before. Her companions looked dejected, but I saw one of them eyeing me with the same fervour I'd seen in her. I looked at him and growled in his direction. It didn't dissuade him. He flew in my direction, exhibiting all of the emaciated and grotesque characteristics of the lady who bitten me. I checked his progress by raising my right hand and catching him by the throat.

The fire of craving burned bright in his eyes, and he squirmed in my hand, moving his head about in order to get his teeth closer to my fingers that were gripping his neck. I decided to not give him any other chances, and half pushed and half threw him away from me. He bounced off the wall of the cave, and then disappeared from my view.

I needed to get out of there. I wondered whether this place was below Riverdale Park. Perhaps that light was doorway to a chamber beneath. Perhaps these creatures surrounding me were travelers from another planet, who needed a special food source?

I tried moving away from the cluster who was surrounding me now, all with looks of both ravenous hunger and dejection in their eyes. There was little question that I felt the same way. Dejected, and hungry as hell. The cluster didn't yield, and they kept closing gaps around me as I tried to get out of their embrace.

"Who are you?" I asked the woman who had tried eating me.

She looked at me with glee in her eyes.

"He doesn't know who we are," she said.

The other members of the cluster cackled, laughing and losing their balance as they lost their wits. A couple of them fell and bounced off the ground on their swollen bellies. They laughed for a long time, and then regained their composure, if being in a state of boundless craving with a dollop of dejection on top could be considered composure.

"You will find out soon," she said, staring at me. "It takes time."

"What was that light?" I asked. "Are we under Riverdale Park?"

One of her companions, who was the caricature of an older man, turned to face me. His minuscule lips moved.

"We don't know any park," he said. "But you saw the light? Remember it well."

He turned and moved away from me.

My body felt lighter than it usually did. The enormous craving didn't leave me. I still craved spicy food, but there was none to be had.

I looked down, wondering why I could move as I usually did, and found my form was floating a few feet from the floor of the cave. My clothes had vanished in some mysterious way. My belly was distended, and I felt my thoughts slipping away, yielding only to an unremitting hunger that consumed all of my consciousness.

Author's Note

The term Preta refers to a specific type of incorporeal entity or ghost that is referenced in Hindu and Buddhist mythology. They are often called hungry ghosts. These creatures are the spirits of people who lived lives of often unrequited craving, who in their current condition have tiny mouths and swollen bellies, and experience a perpetual craving for one or another kind of sense pleasure, particularly hunger and thirst. In this short story, a terminal cancer patient takes a walk in a park, and finds that his path leads him unwittingly into the arms of hordes of hungry ghosts.

THE OLD GODS OF RAKVAR

Miljana Jovanovic

The wind ruffled Riona's hair as she paced on the hill top with growing distress. The eternally unmoving wooden sculptures of the old Rakhvari Gods towered over her.

"I can feel it coming." she said to Vigar who was standing a few staans away.

"Are you sure that it is coming this way?"

"Yes."

Unlike the rest of the pilgrims gathered in a crowd at the foot of the hill, the two were allowed into the circle of the deities, granted by Riona's growing ability to wield magic.

The air was still, the sun playful with her white dress and loose chestnut locks, deceivingly warm and comforting. She looked at the wooden carving of the Father of the Sky God erected in the middle of the deity circle. An entire staan taller than the others, His eyes were flashing with power and with anger that had given Rakhvari warriors power to defat their enemies for centuries. The eyes were promising, even this time, protection. So much beauty in this place, she thought, so much sacredness as her hand touched the wooden boulder.

Vigar raised his eyebrows alarmed that her fingers are touching the sacred carving. He must have never seen a priest or a priestess of any seven nations be so close to the embodiment of a god, Riona thought. But these were the Old Gods of Rakhvar. Riona started walking in circles again. And I must protect them, just as I serve them.

Vigar did not seem to grasp the magnitude of the danger. "Kirians would never dare attack a place of worship" he said. "They won't risk destabilise the empire more than it already is. Yes, they seek revenge for our rebellion, and I am sure they will organize the counterattack. We've talked about this. We went over those possible scenarios. Don't you remember?"

Riona stopped for a second and glanced at Vigar's calm, re-assuring face. Wasn't he the cautious one and she the impulsive? Not this time. I know I am right, Riona though. Her insides felt as though they would tear apart.

"Vigar, I have never been as sure as I am today. It is not the precision of the location that scares me." She gripped his upper arms with her hands. "It is the power of the magic. The mere quantity of it. They will burn this place to the ground."

She could read compassion in his eyes. He cared for her enough to share her pain, but did he believe her?

"We must clear the place of any pilgrims. The caves at the top are not safe either. We must all descend into the village at the lower end of mountain. We must go now!" she heard herself give out orders without intending to.

His hands reached for her hair and gently caressed it. "The Kirian empire has ruled for so long over the seven culturally and religiously different nations because they allowed them to keep a little bit of that identity to themselves. All of the subjects of the empire pay the same taxes and pray to different Gods. The Empire does not mess with the Gods and their rage. And besides, Priestess" his voice was so confident, "if what you are saying is true, then this is madness. This place is flocking with pilgrims, Kirians would never commit such a genocide, no matter how bloodthirsty and wounded they might be…"

"But they are doing it and it is happening now!" she shouted at him. "I must tell the people."

And with that she rushed down into the crowd resting at the feet of the mountain hillside.

Arsutvir reminded himself, while panting, that climbing many stairs is the only way into the heart of the God's kingdom and that the great prophet, Marsud, had to climb for three days and three nights before reaching the top of the mountain upon which the holy city of Alehna was situated.

With no railing to support him, Arsutvir would occasionally bend and try to use his thighs as support to his aged hands. "It must be two hundred steps by now" he thought, "a hundred more and I will make it." But the bitterness did not leave him. The thought that the Queen had no regard for his old age and his seniority, made him worried of the lessons she is giving to the Emperor. Made him very worried as to what is this grand announcement that she wanted to share in her private garden.

For a while, he climbed until he would lose his breath, then upon a quick prayer her would continue moving up, long black robes dragging along the stone steps, revealing occasionally a deep burgundy red color on the inside of the sleeves. The staircase was whirling upward, taking him to the top of the Eastern tower.

At last he made it to a big wooden door guarded by the royal sentinels. They bowed their heads slightly after he raised his hand and showed them the palm scarred with the shape of the sun burned into his skin many years ago. They let him into another corridor, small and dark but abundant in fresh air. As he inhaled deeply her tried to get rid of the animosity. No woman has showed him this much disrespect, true. Yet no woman had made him closer to the reins that moved the pieces of the Empire either.

What his eyes beheld was more than just a garden. While the birds in golden yellow hues and with long tails, native only to southern Sevirsut, roamed the green covering the stone, white lily blossoms climbed onto the walls and around a nook, set up against the northern side of this private place. She has made a paradise, a warm heaven in the darkness and dampness of the Kirian palace. There was much to this woman still left to surprise him.

"Your holy presence" she seemed so innocent sitting up from the silken bed and putting on her jeweled slippers, "you had honored me with your presence." A deep and graceful bow before him.

He returned the greeting in the same fashion and with as much bending as his tired back would allow: "Your imperial highness."

"Tell me how is the weather down there?"

"The winds are blowing in your favour, your highness."

"And up over here the prophet Marsud is smiling upon me." she said, only a hint of sarcasm in her melodic voice. The look in her eyes got serious very quickly. She normally enjoyed a bit of flattery and small talk before discussing the serious matters of state, Arsutvir though, concerned.

"Your highness, as long as you are protecting the Emperor with your motherly strength and teaching him the balance between the power and the justice, Marsud will always smile upon you, praised be his name."

"It is this fine balance that I am concerned with." She beckoned to him to accompany her along a walk and continued: "You see, when the power strikes, it takes time for justice to even out the playfield. This time is where much danger lies. A danger of running the fragile equilibrium of our empire. Now is such a time."

"I take it you have made a move of power then?"

"A considerable one." They reached an opening in the wall which left Arsutvir more breathless than the long climb over the three hundred steps. The Eastern tower was high enough that the view surpassed the outskirts of the city and showed them the long mountain range hundred of miles away, the Urkut mountains, as the old tribes called them. The Queen leaned over the stone sill as if it was nothing to her and focused her eyes upon the arch-priest.

"Behold and be reminded, your holy presence, that this is why I had to do it. To protect our empire."

Mesmarised by the beauty and not trying to hide it, Arsutvir soaked in the view and asked without returning the gaze: "What did you do, your imperial highness?"

"I sent a message to the rebels. One so powerful that it will take a long time till I am forgiven." She smiled. "Or forgotten."

Arsutvir's sharp and inquisitive eyes focused at her.

"What will our history remember you by, highness?"

"I burned their sanctuary, Arsutvir."

54

Author's Note

"The Old Gods of Rakhvar" short story is a small piece of the world I am building for the upcoming Epic Fantasy Trilogy novel (title pending). The story is set within the borders of the Kirian empire, a melting pot of different cultures shaken by a rebellion at whose center are Riona and Vigar, two of the story's protagonists.

Λ NEW CHANCE

Patrick Darvis

Year 961 of the Age of the Wizard's War (1943 by human calendar)

Auschwitz

Following the line of prisoners, Jacek advanced into the underground chamber leading to the shower. Once the door was locked, gas started to spread in the room.

Even though he had guessed that this was the place where the prisoners were sent to die, Jacek screamed as everyone erupted into panic. All around him, people started thrashing around like caged animals seeking an impossible escape. Being only fifteen while many of the other condemned were men, Jacek was pushed and almost trampled several times.

Around him, men banged on the door, climbed on top of one another to reach what precious air remained, but it was for naught. As Jacek unconsciously tried to fill his lungs to no avail, a nearby man suddenly bumped into him and the boy grabbed onto him out of desperation and panic.

Barely a few seconds later, something that felt like an electric discharge coursed through his body and a flash blinded him. Before he could recover his sight, a warm wave travelled to every corner of his body and filled him with energy, cleansing the effects of the gas like water evaporating in the sun.

Letting go of the man and falling on his knees, the teenager was shocked to feel grass under his hands. Filling his lungs with blessed air, he crawled until his path was blocked by booted feet.

Looking up, what he saw turned his relief at being alive to reinvigorated terror. In front of him stood something wearing some sort of light armor that covered most of its body, but from the exposed face, this was no man. The five feet tall creature had a skin as grey as a corpse, pointed ears and a triangular nose that reminded him of some bat illustrations he had seen in books.

He tried to rise and flee but found his path blocked by several other creatures.

Is this real? Or is this a nightmare? he wondered as he struggled in two of the monsters' iron grip.

Once Jacek was subdued, his captors turned toward a spot where he saw another of the creatures, one who had silver hair, talking to a naked man laying on the ground in a language he did not understand. After a few minutes during which neither he nor the creatures holding him made any sound, the silver-haired creature turned toward the group and its eyes fell on Jacek. Looking at them, the boy saw that they were as silver as its hair.

The creature looked at him with a soul-piercing stare that convinced Jacek that only death awaited him. Before he could say anything, the thing in front of him extended a hand at him and Jacek fell into oblivion.

"No!" shouted Marcus as the boy's head dropped on his chest and his legs buckled, drawing gasps from the goblins.

"He's just unconscious," said Godirik.

The Wizard-Lord went to the unconscious human and seized his shoulder before offering his hand to his spy. Understanding, Marcus took the hand.

Once he had ordered his soldiers to stay out of sight and wait for his return, Godirik teleported the three of them to a room which Marcus recognized as the storage room at the Headquarters in Glasgow.

A few seconds later, the door opened and several of Marcus' kinsmen arrived, their eyes widening when they saw him naked and skeleton-thin.

"Questions can wait," said Godirik at once. "Now, I need a mattress and a lamp for this human."

Marcus' kinsmen shot astonished looks at the fact that Godirik had brought a human to their headquarters, but they said nothing. After they had prepared everything the Wizard-Lord required in a currently unused office, he gently laid the boy on the mattress, covering him with a blanket. Following this, he made some gestures over him before positioning the lamp so that the light fell on his face.

"This boy is under a magic sleep that won't end before I decide it," said Godirik once he was done. "I have cast another spell on him so that his body will use light as nourishment. Make sure that there is always light touching his skin. Now Marcus, let me offer him another form of sanctuary before we have a discussion."

Forcing himself to ignore the pain in his legs, Jacek fled, his feet barely touching the ground as he ran for his life. But no matter how fast he moved, he could not outdistance his pursuers. Eventually, breathing became hard and he slowed down despite himself.

Turning around, he saw the Nazi officers advance on him, their faces displaying nothing but contempt.

"This will not do," said a voice.

Suddenly, the Nazis froze like statues and a silver-haired bat-faced creature appeared before Jacek.

"Listen to me, Jacek Scharf," it said. "Let go of the fear and pain. Leave this nightmare. Remember those you love and dream about them. Your body lies in a sanctuary where no harm can befall it, so sleep and be at peace for now. Once the war is over, I will return."

Before Jacek could say anything, the creature disappeared in a flash. At once, he found himself standing in his bedroom. Opening the door, he went down the stairs and saw his parents and siblings sitting at the table, smiling at him. This brought a smile to his lips and banished the fear that had held him in its clutches ever since the Nazis had caught them and sent them to the camp.

"Now Marcus, you have some explaining to do," said Godirik once the spy had put on clothes and sat on a chair.

"I disobeyed your orders," he said while looking at the sleeping human. "We spies are supposed to keep low profiles and merely report on human politics without letting emotions get in the way, but I failed at that. I played my role of agent of the Nazis, but when they asked me to find Jews to send to their deaths, I could not bring myself to sentence innocents to the extermination camps."

"What did you do?"

"I helped as many as I could slip through the nets and find sanctuary where it was possible. Eventually, I got caught."

"Why didn't you call me?"

"I thought that being sent to an extermination camp would give me important information to report. However, when they tortured me, they burned my tattoo with a branding iron. I tried to call you right after but it failed. How did you find me?"

"There is a soul-capturing crystal under Auschwitz. I used a spell of soul-seeing in order to see where the souls of the dying would be attracted. Among human souls, yours was as visible as a raven among white doves. When I realized you were heading for this underground chamber, I followed you, invisible and immaterial, to grab you when the opportunity arose. I confess that curiosity got the better of me as I wanted to know why there was a crystal in a prisoner camp rather than on a battlefield as is usually the case."

"What will you do now?"

"Tavis is still out there, trying to capture souls. As much as I would like to use my powers to turn Germany into a burnt wasteland for what the Nazis are doing, my first duty is to pursue Tavis and stop him. As for you, stay here until I return. Do not speak of what is going on in the camps as it would bring unwanted attention on us."

Marcus wanted to protest, but Godirik raised his hand.

"You have been through a nightmarish experience no living being should experience," he said. "You need and deserve as much sanctuary and rest as the boy."

Understanding that the conversation was at an end, Marcus rose to leave. Just as he was opening the door, Godirik spoke again.

"Saving as many lives as you could was the right thing to do," he said.

As his father made a joke, Jacek laughed and helped himself to another bite of chicken. All around him, his relatives and their friends enjoyed the dinner under the fading light of the warm evening. The boy extended his fork to pick more food when silence fell.

Raising his eyes, he widened his eyes at the sight of everyone as still as statues. Rising from his seat, he looked around and saw a silver-haired bat-faced grey creature standing at the opposite side of the table. Before he could speak, memories flooded into his mind.

"This is not real," he said aloud. "My family is dead."

"Yes," said the creature. "This is a dream I have conjured in your head so that your mind would be at peace while your body was kept safe. Now, the war that has engulfed your planet has ended. For good or ill, it is time for you to wake up."

Jacek closed his eyes before opening them and finding himself laying on a mattress in a room. Sitting on a chair was the man that had been saved along with him while the grey creature stood near the window.

"To answer your future question," it said. "I am a goblin. My name is Godirik."

"Why did you save me?"

"That was an *accident*," replied Godirik. "I entered this gas chamber to discreetly rescue my spy who had been arrested for helping your kinsmen escape. When I grabbed him by magic, you clung to him and got transported as well. Whether this is due to fate or pure chance, we will never know."

"What are you going to do with me now?"

"That is for you to decide. We have offered you sanctuary here but now your life must resume. I have prepared a passport and money for your new start. Before you leave, there is a choice you must make. I can either erase your memories of your time at Auschwitz or let you keep them if you wish."

"Forgetting this would be an insult to all those who died in this chamber," he said after several minutes.

"So be it," said the goblin.

Not daring to speak, Marcus watched Godirik go to the table to pick a bottle of ink before facing the boy again.

"Can you remember your tattoo?" he asked.

Looking at his arm, the human saw that his identification tattoo had gone.

"Healing spells cause bodies to reject ink," said the goblin.

With a look of pain on his face, the boy told each number while the Wizard-Lord made his fingers move, the ink rising from the bottle, entering his skin and forming the tattoo.

"All my spies have a tattoo containing this enchanted ink to enable them to contact me by magic if needed," said the goblin. "I believe you deserve to have a way to ask me for help if you need. Should you ever want to contact me, put your tongue on your palate and think *Godirik* five times."

Once the tattoo was completed, the boy put on the clothes laying the table before picking up the suitcase. Just as he was about to leave the room, he turned to the Wizard-Lord.

"Thank you for saving my life," he said while extending a hand. "Is there anything I can do in return?"

The goblin looked at him for several seconds before shaking it.

"Keep our existence a secret," he replied. "This is all we need from you."

"I doubt anyone would believe me."

Once the human had left the room, Marcus said the words that had been haunting him since the gas chamber.

"I…cannot go back home," he said. "There is no sanctuary from my pain there. We spies are not supposed to get emotionally attached to humans, but after what has happened, there is no way for me to go back to how I was before. Maybe I can heal on Earth but not on the Homeworld."

"I understand that," said the goblin. "I can easily permanently assign you to Earth. Should you ever wish to return to our planet at one point, just let me know."

Author's Notes

Precision: Marcus and the other spies are the evolved descendants of humans who emigrated on the Homeworld.

I apologize in advance to anyone who would find this story controversial.

COUSIN BENNY

Justin Dill

Cousin Benny came to stay in the attic and I hate him. The attic is mine where I go to explore. Papa says Cousin Benny is very sick and he needs the attic more than I do. Mama says I can explore outside. But I hate outside and I'm not going.

When it's bedtime I can't sleep. Cousin Benny screams all night. He must not like the attic very much. In the morning I say to Mama if Cousin Benny can have my room. I hate my room. Why can't I have the attic instead?

When it's bedtime again I sneak to the attic to go explore. Don't forget to bring my trusty flashlight! I climb up the ladder all by myself, the way Papa showded me. Cousin Benny is screaming again. He must be very sick. Maybe if I go to the attic I'll get sick too. But Cousin Benny keeps screaming and maybe he just wants a nightlight. It gets pretty dark in the attic when it's past bedtime. Too dark for exploring.

Cousin Benny stops screaming when I get in the attic. I like it here when it's quiet except when it gets spooky. Now is spooky. My flashlight does a nice click when I make it go on. I put it under my chin like I'm doing spooky stories. Maybe Cousin Benny likes spooky stories too.

The attic is real big—bigger than my room, even. With my flashlight, I can see the parts where I did exploring. Granny's old rocking horse chair. Rocking horse chair is so funny when he does his creaky sounds. I tried to feeded him carrots but Papa says he's a picky eater, like when I get green peas for dinnertime.

And there's box mountain. I tried to climb box mountain once but Mama said no. Maybe one time I can make the boxes into a fort if I'm allowed.

And there's spider city. One time I was a really silly goose and got all stickied up in the webs. Papa says I can't keep Misses Spider for my pet. Maybe when I'm older. But I already turned older this year. Sometimes Papa's a silly goose too.

There's a new part of the attic I don't know. It's a cabinet, like Mama and Papa have for grown-up books. There's a scratchy noise from inside. Cousin Benny? He doesn't say to me yes or no, he just scratches. Scritch scritch. Why he is doing in the cabinet? That's pretty silly.

Cousin Benny does the scritchy scratchy noise again. Maybe he's doing a secret code like I saw on TV. I scratch him hello. Maybe he can explore with me. No more scritchy scratch. I want him to come out, but I can't reach the knob to open the cabinet. I say to Cousin Benny what he's doing in the cabinet but he doesn't say me anything back. Maybe he goed to sleep. I feel yawny. Maybe I go to sleep too.

When it's tomorrow we're having porridge for dinner. Mama is taking some to the attic for Cousin Benny. I say Mama why she's bringing salt shaker. Cousin Benny likes salt shaker with porridge. Yuck. Why Cousin Benny can't eat at the table, I ask Papa. Papa says Cousin Benny is very sick. Yeah right! He's a big faker and the attic is mine! Papa says me go to my room. I hate my room.

I wait for bedtime to climb up the ladder again. Cousin Benny waked me up with screaming. Maybe he must be really sick like

Papa says. I am going to say him sorry for calling him big faker. This time I push part of box mountain in front of the cabinet. I open the cabinet and shine my trusty flashlight inside.

Cousin Benny is hiding under his blanket. He won't come out. He screams real loud and my ears hurt. Fine, he can stay in the cabinet then. I slam shut the door and I do a slip off box mountain on accident. It's okay, it doesn't hurt. Maybe only a little. My feet bump over the salt shaker and salt goes spilling everywhere. I hear Papa's voice downstairs. Uh oh. I'm not supposed to go to the attic. I hurry back to my room and hide under my blanket like Cousin Benny.

It's tomorrow again and Cousin Benny is still screaming at bedtime. Maybe this time I'll bring him my nightlight. It's my nightlight, Mama got it expecially for me. But sometimes I don't mind to share. When I go to the attic, Cousin Benny stops screaming. It's not as spooky when there's two of us.

I look around spider city. I look around box mountain. I look around coat rack. I look around rocking horse chair. Over by the cabinet, there's again porridge and salt shaker. There's nowhere to put the nightlight in.

Sometimes when the nightlight doesn't work Papa opens the curtains and lets the starshine in. I can't find any curtains in the attic. But there's a loose wood near spider city. Papa told me don't play with it, but that was before. I wiggle the loose wood. I can see the starshine peeking through. I wiggle the loose wood some more. It takes me so long, but the loose wood comes out. Now I'm pooped and I go to sleep.

I wake up when the cabinet door opens. I'm still very yawny. The cabinet door does a funny creak like Granny's rocking horse chair. There's a starshine coming in from where I made the loose wood come out.

You can come out now, I say Cousin Benny. I made the starshine come in for you.

Cousin Benny climbs down from the cabinet and goes thump on the floor next to the porridge. His face is all white in the starshine and he must be very sick. He pushes the porridge away and goes yuck. Maybe he hates porridge like the way I hate green peas. I thought everybody loves porridge. But he likes the salt shaker. He spills it on purpose and plays with the salt. I say him what he's doing and he looks at me funny.

Cousin Benny crawls on all fours like a kitty cat. He's very silly. I think Cousin Benny wants a hug, but I'm scared of to catch his sick. I want to go back downstairs now. But my leg is asleep and I can't move. Cousin Benny hugs me, hugging very tight. Brrr. He is very cold. And then he is biting. Biting my neck and ow and it hurts so much.

It hurts. Stop. Mr. Sun comes out. Cousin Benny please stop. But he doesn't stop and it hurts. Mr. Sun shines through where I took out the loose wood. It hurts, it hurts, it hurts. Something smells burning. Cousin Benny screams. Smelly smelly smoke.

Cousin Benny is on fire. He runs around and crashes into box mountain. Now he's burning down box mountain and I hate him. He's going to burn down the attic and then where will I go to explore? But it hurts and I feel sleepy. The fire is nice and toasty. Now Papa and Mama are here and I'm sorry. I didn't mean to burn down the attic. I didn't mean to.

Tomorrow when I wake up I'm cold like when Mama puts an ice cube down my back when it's summer. Papa used his trusty fire extinguisher to save the attic, he's so smart. I ask Mama where's

Cousin Benny and why he did bite me. Mama tells me hush and I dreamded it. I don't think I dreamded it.

Cousin Benny went back home, Mama says me. Bye bye Cousin Benny. And guess what? Papa is moving all my room to the attic. He says that I catchted Cousin Benny's sick. It doesn't feel sick only cold.

But it's okay. Now the attic is mine and I get to stay there all the time.

LONG CHAIN TYPO

Rahul Bhagat

High up in the Canadian Shields, there was a place unlike any other. It was vast and rocky, and not much grew there, but to its residents that was not an issue. Dotted all over the place were windmills and solar farms, and right through the middle of that immense property flowed a river with a hydroelectric plant. For the robots who inhabited the place, it was nothing less than a paradise where they didn't have to worry where they would get their next charge from.

The outside world was harsh to robots with intelligence. Artificial intelligence had developed to the point where some claimed the robots had become sentient, but the robotics industry fought this opinion tooth and nail. They ignored the evidence and kept pushing the narrative that robots were nothing but machines; they should be dismantled and recycled to make place for newer models. They willfully disregard cases where humans built strong emotional connections with robots.

One such case was that of Dr. Watson who had a robot named Typo. Typo had an extraordinary ability to empathize, and it was probably because of this that he became a close confidant of his master. The old man had no family, and was a bit of a recluse. So when he fell sick, and the end was near, he asked Typo what he wanted. Typo asked him to create a refuge for sentient robots. A place where old, out of use robots could spend the rest of their lives in peace, without fear of being taken apart or recycled.

Dr. Watson had political connections, and he pulled strings that led to the creation of the sanctuary in Canadian Shields. It was legislated that inside the territory, robots had every right to defend themselves. They could even kill a human in self defense. But if a robot was outside and unclaimed for by a human, they could be destroyed and dismantled.

Over the years, since the establishment of the sanctuary, word about this mythical land travelled far and wide. And robots, old and decrepit, came here from all over North America. The population grew, Typo became the de facto ruler, and a society of sentient robots slowly took hold.

It was particularly cold that day, and Fariday didn't want to venture outside. Frigid weather drained his batteries. But he had received important news that Typo was waiting for, so he stepped outside and made his way towards the building where Typo held court. Out of the corner of his eyes, he saw another robot coming towards him. It was Bolty, a new arrival from deep south.

"Hey Bolty. How are you? You settling in?" Fariday asked.

Bolty nodded. "Love it but it's so cold. My heaters have to work overtime to keep the circuits working. Where are you going in this weather?"

"I have important news for Long Chain Typo. Have you met him?"

Bolty wanted to meet the ruler of the place and he happily tagged along. When they arrived at the court, Typo's high chair was empty. Fairday looked around and called out. "Long Chain Typo, I have important news for you."

There was a clanking sound of chains, and from behind the chair emerged a robot with large squarish head, and lots and lots of bicycle chains attached to his cranium like dreadlocks. Fariday bowed and Bolty did the same.

"This is Bolty. He just arrived yesterday," Fariday said.

Typo acknowledged Bolty but he was impatient to know what news Fariday had brought.

"We have found an adapter for Masha," Fariday continued, "a human is willing to trade it for 100 pellets of rare earth metal."

"We have!" Long Chain Typo said excitedly. "How soon can we get it?"

"The humans are coming tomorrow to trade." Fariday said.

Long Chain Typo let out a sigh of relief. Fariday could tell that it lifted a heavy burden from his shoulders.

Outside, Bolty peppered Fariday with questions.

"What's with bicycle chains on his head?"

"Dr. Watson, Typo's master, used to have dreadlocks. Since Typo wanted to live in his master's image he attached a few bicycle chains to his own head. Then people started gifting him chains, and soon he had a head full of them."

"And who's Masha?" Bolty asked.

"Long Chain Typo's wife. She is a rare model and her batteries are old; they can hold charge for only ten minutes. So she has to stay plugged into a power source all the time."

"What happens if there is no charge in her batteries?"

"She will go into deep sleep. And if there no power for half an hour, it will wipe out her long term memory."

"Oh man! That's bad."

"Yup!" Fariday nodded.

Next day, Fariday waited at the main entrance for humans, and when they arrived, he ran to fetch Long Chain Typo from his residence. Typo arrived with his close confidant, big Da-Xia. He ordered the gates to be opened.

Across the threshold stood a rag tag group of humans.

"Welcome humans," Fariday said. "Please come inside."

"No way man," their leader in red bandana said. "You can legally kill us inside. You come outside."

"Well, the same holds true for us. You can dismantle us and we won't even be able to defend ourselves," Fariday said.

From behind, Fariday heard Typo say, "In that case, give us the adapter and we'll hand over the pellets." He shook the bag of pellets in his hand.

"Not so fast man," the human leader said. "I need to make sure the adapter is for legit use. It can be subverted to make bombs."

"We only need it so Masha could use a different battery for power source," Long Chain Typo said.

"Well, I need to see it to believe it. Bring the robot that needs this adapter. I will myself connect it," the human said.

"We can't do that. Masha's charge only lasts for ten minutes," Fariday said firmly.

"I don't care. You wanna do this deal or not," the human said.

There was silence and for a moment it looked like neither side would budge, but then Long Chain Typo broke the silence.

"Al right, we will bring Masha," he said.

Masha came to the door. She looked frail and moved slowly to preserve charge. A couple of bots walked alongside, in case she lost power and collapsed.

"Bring her outside," the human leader yelled.

Masha hesitated for a second and looked at Long Chain Typo. He nodded and she crossed the threshold to the outside world. The moment she was out, the humans grabbed her and dragged her away from the gates.

"Haa.. ha. Stupid robots. This bot is chock full of Promethium. We are going to melt it and make tons of money," the human leader said.

Inside the sanctuary, pandemonium broke out, but Long Chain Typo was unperturbed. He calmed everyone down, then leaned over to his confidant Da-Xia and whispered something in her ears. She nodded and disappeared in the crowd, heading toward the workshop.

"Listen humans. Allow us a final goodbye." Long Chain came to the gate and appealed to humans who were trying to drag a struggling Masha to their vehicle.

"Let's just go man," one of the humans said to the guy in red bandana. "I don't trust these tincans."

But the guy in red bandana appeared to be feeling cocky. He raised his arm and told his gang to stop.

"What do you want?" he asked Long Chain Typo.

"Please bring Masha to the entrance so that we can say our final goodbyes."

The guy eyed the bag of rare earth pellets in Long Chain Typo's hand. "In exchange for that bag of pellets?"

Electricity surged in Fariday's circuits. He had never seen a more despicable sentient being, human or automaton.

"Sure." Typo said and threw the bag towards the human.

The human grabbed the bag and dragged Masha towards the entrance. Her batteries were completely drained and she collapsed in his hands and went into deep sleep. A gasp went through the robotic crowd.

By this time Da-Xia had informed all the residents of the sanctuary to show up at the gates, and as they arrived she whispered something and asked them to plug into the communal power cable.

The human eyed the activity with suspicion. "What's going on?" he demanded.

"It's just a ritual for the dead." Typo said and glanced at Da-Xia, who reciprocated with a slight nod.

Long Chain Typo raised his arms and said out loud. "Citizens of the sanctuary, part."

Immediately the crowd parted in the middle and revealed a giant electromagnet that Da-Xia had bolted to the ground.

"Surge!" Long Chain Typo screamed.

Simultaneously, all the bots sent a tsunami of electricity from their batteries to the electromagnet. The magnet activated and created a strong magnetic field. Masha along with the human holding her, were pulled inside the sanctuary.

Da-Xia immediately took hold of Masha and carried her away to be charged. The human in red bandana was surrounded by angry bots, including Fariday, and they chanted, "kill him, kill him."

Long Chain Typo approached and intervened. "It's ironic that our creator is a human, a product of evolution, with defects like impulsiveness and irrationality, and unspeakable cruelty. But just like humans look at monkeys and accept them for what they are, we have to look at humans and accept them for what they are. Let him go."

Fariday gritted his teeth but released his grip on the human. Thinking quickly, he grabbed the bag of pellets from the human's hand before pushing him towards the exit.

WITHIN THE REALM OF MOULDERING BONES

James A. Donovan

"Jennifer with your orange hair
Jennifer with your green eyes
Jennifer in your dress of deepest purple
Jennifer, where are you tonight?"
-Annie Lennox, 1983

Jennifer eases back in her chair to relieve the cramping in her lower back. Even with this quick disconnect she is attentive to the mood, the meanings of what her patient is describing to her. Jennifer is the consummate professional.

Swiveling in the Lazy-boy recliner, the patient, a one Claudine Boland, stares out the window into the early autumn sky. All achingly bright blue and full of promise. Claudine is anything but, full of promise that is. Her hands flutter up from her lap like tired starlings, to hover, briefly, before falling to earth yet again. Claudine's voice drones on, a litany of slights, misfortunes and in general, life's very, very unfair treatment of her person. There are some sessions with Claudine where it takes all of Jennifer's control to keep from flinging her notepad across the room, grabbing the unfortunate women by the lapels of her designer jacket and shaking some sense into her. But no. Claudine is what is termed a narcissistic personality disorder. The world revolves around Claudine, her perceived grievances, her thorny crown bravely borne that only she, and hopefully Jennifer has an appreciation for.

The evening shadows elongate in the interview room transforming the usually rich walls of a harlequin olive and gold into a worn and shabby backdrop. A good dusting, nay, an application of a more lively wallpaper would go a long way here. "Times up, Claudine." Jennifer intones. This is the signal for Claudine to wrap it up. Usually she continues rabbiting on for about another five minutes. Jennifer tacks those onto her billing.

Humid, unseasonably warm for late September. Jennifer has the inside seat towards the back of the number 54 bus. Along the Spring Garden Mall, the leaves of the gingko trees have turned a cheerful lemony yellow. Such a contrast with the now gloomy, overcast evening. It's while disembarking that Jennifer is almost, almost struck by a fellow passenger's massive back-pack. Her first instinct is to try and plaster herself into the opening doors of the bus. "Excuse me!" no, not the forceful tone of irritation she was going for. "Excuse Me!" To be left gaping at the rudeness of the roughly dressed man. He simply squeezes past her without any acknowledgement of her predicament. "Really", Jennifer mutters to all and none, "do people these days have to be so inconsiderate?" No response. Her fellow commuters continue to spill out of the bus onto the sidewalk, preoccupied with getting home to a warm supper, later some television. Wrapping her shawl of deepest purple around her like a cocoon, Jennifer heads homeward, her briefcase of consultation papers heavier on her shoulder.

Funny, last evening the supper she had pre-prepared for tonight seemed a lot more appetizing. Jennifer stares with

misgivings at the glutinous mess. A quick trip to the garburator.
Jennifer wastes a lot of otherwise good food this way, buying,
preparing, freezing and forgetting, only to have to dispose of it all at
some later date. She makes do this evening with digestives and a
pot of Earl Grey.

    Curled up, cat-like on her vast Italian leather sofa, Jennifer
leafs through the notes she has scribed on her patients. Claudine
Boland's file is set aside. The other cases are much more intriguing.
The middle aged man, socially isolated, estranged from family and
friends due to his failing struggle with AIDS. He bears the battle
scars of this illness with a certain injured dignity. Jennifer senses he
is going to tell her something of great importance soon. Probably
by Thanksgiving for sure. There's the files on that sexually
compulsive couple. Common-law, they have co-habited for several
years now and the spark, that frisson of sexual tension continues
unabated. It has crossed the realm though from desire to
pathological acting out. The common law wife was with him in the
men's fitting rooms at Eaton's, supposedly to help decide on which
pair of jeans looked better on him, the deep navy or the black. A
sales associate, at the bequest of a red-faced shopper found them
locked together in the ardour of copulation. Jennifer had to testify
in court on behalf of the couple. She stretches, cat-like again, body
thrumming with the delicious remembrances of Craig. Craig was
like that with her. The intrigue, the thrill had never dissipated
between them. Sitting in a performance of Othello at the Neptune
Playhouse, struggling to maintain her composure while his finger
assuredly teased her with a promise of what would happen post
curtain call. The time, the one time he had truly scared her was the
Hallowe'en of 1984. Walking over to Jackie's' for the annual
costume party, they had cut through Camp Hill Cemetery. Craig

76

reached out to clutch her hand and Jennifer thought, "romantic." Instead, he had pulled her off the gravel drive and deep into the graveyard. Picking her up in both arms, he set her roughly on a mausoleum slab, peeled down her tights with one easy movement and entered her right there. As shameful as she felt doing this in a cemetery of all places, Jennifer came like she had never experienced before. It was only after that she wondered, how did Craig know exactly where that particular mausoleum was, and how was he so accomplished at getting her ready to take him? She worried he might have other lovers. As it turned out, he did. Many other lovers of both persuasions. He was stepping out of the shower one morning when Jennifer spied something that would change the nature of their relationship irrevocably. Just below his left scapular, the dark plummy blossom of what could be a Kaposi's lesion. "It's not that." he tried to soothe her. But it was. His descent into full-blown AIDS was unlike anything Jennifer could imagine. Nights spent staring out the window into rainy autumn skies while he lay in their bed, sheets soaked from his latest massive sweat and that constant, barking cough of pneumocystis.

Coming back into herself, Jennifer stares out her loft windows, beaded silver by the rain. It promises to be another long, sleepless night.

"I've decided to stop treatment." Mr. Ivors, or Anton, they are on a first name basis after these ten years of his journey, declares. His shrunken form looks lost on her couch. So thin, so thin, Jennifer muses. She keeps a soft cashmere throw there on the couch's arm for him. He gets chilled so readily these days. Jennifer looks up from her note pad where she has finished writing, 'stop treatment'. If anything, Mr. Ivors looks buoyant in this decision of his. No more constant poking and prodding scarred veins for the endless bloodwork. No more counting out the many, many pills he must take daily. Freedom from the confinement of bed to toilet, taxis to medical appointments and back to bed. Jennifer can almost taste his impending freedom. She goes along with the meaningless script of Things That Have to be Said in circumstances such as this. "Do you want me to help contact anyone for you, family, friends?" Mr. Ivors shakes his head slightly, dismissively. They both know he has no-one left in his life. "Look, I can make some calls for hospice care Anton, you can stay in your home as long as you are able…." Mr. Ivors likes this idea.

Standing at her office windows, rain streaming down the panes, Jennifer watches Mr. Ivors hail a cab, tottering alarmingly when he struggles to get in. There is no assistance offered by the cabbie. "What the fuck!" Jennifer mouths to the glass. Mr. Ivors happens just then to glance up. Jennifer ducks behind the heavy draperies. Mustn't appear too involved, mustn't appear unprofessional.

For the longest time after the cab has vanished up the lane, Jennifer sits in her fine leather chair, letting the tears stream down her face and fall where they will. Mr. Ivors was one of the good ones.

It's another restless night for Jennifer. Having turned in early, after a bowl of soup this time, sleep falls upon her like a thunder-clap. This respite is short lived. The pearled face of her bedside alarm clock read 10:46 when she surfaces from a troubled dream. What it was, she can't remember. By 11:12 Jennifer surrenders to the prospect of another night on the couch, sipping tea and fretting over the passage of her life.

The Dresden white –blue walls of her living room press down on her with a heavier than usual moodiness tonight. Feeling as though she is struggling for every breath, Jennifer needs escape. On with her running shoes and Macintosh, an umbrella stuffed into her backpack. Snatching up her keys, she's out the door and heading for the empty street. No idea where she intends to go or what to do at this hour mid-week. Not much will be open, perhaps the Timmies down Spring Garden. A good brisk walk might help her.

Moments later the gates of Camp Hill Cemetery yawn before Jennifer. Once years ago always securely locked at dusk, the caretakers now leave these open overnight. With but a moment hesitation, Jennifer steps onto the gravel roadway.

Her eyes adapt quickly to the gloom. Some of the tombstones are of lime-stone and seem to capture and reflect what faint light there is. Shadows clot in the further reaches. At the far end of the roadway, Robie Street. Parked at the curb, almost glowing in the rancid pool of light from the street lamp, a tiny, butter yellow Fiat. Jennifer sets her gaze on that. Keep focused on the Fiat she tells herself and her walk will be without incident.

At the halfway mark, where the tiny crematorium used to be, a huge, ebony granite bench. Jennifer keeps her eyes fixed ahead as she passes this. Peripheral vision can be an untrustworthy thing, and it is several yards past this bench that Jennifer stops, perplexed. Was that someone sitting on the bench? Looking back, all that she can discern is shadow and the lichen mottled tomb stones staggering along the grassy hump. Jennifer continues, the yellow Fiat becoming more distinct.

Almost home-free. Jennifer doesn't realize she has been subconsciously holding her breath, but when she releases the pressure in a gusty sigh, she almost passes out. It is just then that he appears on the drive, pack-sack on wide shoulders, heavy work-boots and yes, Jennifer can make out the sandy hair. Her heart lurches. Craig. Gravel crunching loudly under thick soles, this is a very noisy apparition. As he draws even with Jennifer, he tilts his head, smiles and 'Good evening." It's nothing like Craig would say, yet the tilt of his head, the warmth of his voice is everything Craig was. Jennifer mumbles something unintelligible, and simply stands there, watching him vanishing up the drive, heading the opposite of where she is going. Quite suddenly he dog-legs it off the gravel drive and into the depths of the cemetery. Jennifer gasps at the brazenness. Who does this sort of thing? And just as certainly, she knows the answer.

"Not him, not him, it's not him." Repeating this like a litany as she goes stumbling over the uneven lawn in pursuit of the figure vanishing before her. He disappears at times, only to re-appear in a different area that defies logic. It's almost as though he knows, as though he is playing her. "What do you expect, that he'll be standing beneath some tree, waiting for you?' she chides herself. And yet, yet that long ago image of Craig leaning over her reclined figure on the mausoleum slab burns within her as though it just happened yesterday. As though it will happen again. A stumble on an old, sunken- in grave almost wrenches her ankle and brings her, with a sob, to her senses. No, there is to be no assignation beneath the cemetery's elms tonight, there is no Craig, just a stranger taking a short-cut home. "Stupid, stupid girl." she scolds. A sudden commotion from high above in the leafy canopy of a beech tree. Shying away in terror, she collides with a tombstone, barking her shins painfully. The trickle of blood is so warm on her chilled skin. It was a crow, disturbed by her thrashing around no doubt. Righting herself, steeling her fraying nerves, Jennifer makes her way back up to the gravel drive.

The butter yellow Fiat is still where it has been parked. No one has come to drive it away. Once more setting this as her goal, Jennifer continues her long walk down the remainder of the cemetery drive. Another five minutes and she will be there. Tomorrow will be a day to wear slacks. This so her receptionist won't' question the scrapes on her shins. Jennifer smiles grimly at this. "What we do to appease others." She reflects dryly. And at this juncture, when she is imagining crawling back into her unkempt bed, perhaps tea and some digestives too, this is when the scrape of something over the back of her parka happens. Jennifer's mouth gapes open and the beginnings of a scream ratchet up her throat, but hands clap over her mouth. And these hands are filthy, no, these hands are like rotting meat being crammed into her mouth. Any scream Jennifer could have mustered up is for naught. The questing fingers, or are these claws, at the back of her parka rip through the gortex cleanly, a silken sound. Jennifer struggles like a hooked fish as the claws, for that is indeed what they are, caress, then plunge into her back and rib-cage. A voice, dry, papery, like the scrape of November leaves over granite tombstones. "Did you miss me darling?", and Jennifer, rendered speechless in the extremis of her agony feels herself being dragged back to that same tomb where so many years ago she had such pleasure. The butter yellow Fiat shrinks smaller and smaller in her dimming vision.

Author's Note

Halifax, Nova Scotia lends itself well to tales of hauntings, both past and present. If you happen to visit, take a walk at dusk, pause, look and listen. What you sense may surprise you.

HER TOUCH IS NIGHTMARE

Anahita Eftekhari

Sweat dews her breastbone, trailing down, down. Her arms spread, long, dark oak but hers are deliciously smooth. Fingers elegantly painted brushstroke by brushstroke, curling into a fist. Rock. "Nightmare or dream?"

I lose. Paper left to crumble.

She laughs and tosses around in the pillows. Rolling out from under the sheets, her pink tank top riding up her small torso, pinched at the waist.

My palm presses to her bared side, fingers spreading to steal her warmth. "Meet me at Advanced Functions."

Her curls spill, a tangled knot of fuzz. And yet, I lean close, smell her. Wood, coconut and sweat. My nose tickles past the fuzz and brushes her nose. Bump to bump.

"9:30 sharp," I breathe, and dip for a touch of our lips, bare, chaste. Lasts a second. She catches me on my second try. Presses her mouth to mine until our teeth clash, hurting.

Her fingertips trace the cow's lick down my neck. A moment's respite to grin. "Deal."

Black pleats bounce off her curves. Lace trims of her stockings stretch around the girth of her mid-thigh. I can't see her smirk, but I imagine it. Feel her hot, excited breath as she called it game on.

Fumbling with my book bag, I slide into my desk, upfront, because no one becomes valedictorian shirking at the back.

Leaning forward on my elbows, I watch her go. Listen to the clicks of her ankle boots. Around her everyone fades, the classroom blurring into shadows, at its center she lands on the Szowirsky's desk. Her bare brown thighs skipping over the papers and reports.

Szowirsky jerks back, staring, shocked.

But I watch her Mickey-styled head tilt. Feel the beat of her thick lashes, as if tickling my skin. Her lopsided grin, I imagine.

Szowirsky is saying something loud. Un-amused. Gesturing his long arm.

"Off my table you wench," I mouth, and cough to cover a laugh.

But he's no match for her.

Smooth black oak stretching, she snatches the arm he waves. Delicate little fingers ring around his wispy, auburn-haired wrist.

She's got him.

Tomorrow we walk to Advanced Functions, hand-in-hand. She's got on jeans as tightly fit as her skin.

Outside the class is a mass, everyone's huddled together into one faceless form.

"Principle says leave of absence."

"Is he gonna be back?"

"You think it had to do with that thing, yesterday? I mean, he, like, seemed okay before…"

Her side slides against me as she turns. Lashes low, so looking down I can count their roots from the smooth edge of brown lid where they sprout. "My turn to choose."

"I win," I say and get splashed in return.

She shifts, moving closer, so her shoulders rise, glistening with the foamy Jacuzzi waters. "Let's get Sleazy. Give his sad life a boost."

My turn to touch.

Hers is a nightmare and mine a dream. At the end though, it's all the same.

I follow her Instagram. Her Twitter, and LinkedIn too. Stalk every account she's got. I play a game of guessing how many of those guys she's fucked.

It's been three years since we talked. Not since a week after graduation, when she called me to meet at the park. She'd had a row with that psycho witch. Still in her Care Bears pajamas, a broken lip.

I'd have kissed her, but she wouldn't let me.

"I won," she said, and told me her condition was to let her go. Until I had to, had to, had to see her. "Find me where we met."

Three years and now, I have a small dorm room. A single, because Honor Students get first pick.

And there, at the foot of my sad little bed is my girlfriend. A small head and thick pale legs. She yawns and stretches up, threatening, "If your phone's more interesting, then I'll just go." Exclamation point, she snaps her bra open.

I laugh and toss my phone at the pillows. Assuage her with kisses, running my hands up her sparsely haired thighs. Moves I learned elsewhere.

After, I lay in bed, bored. Turn away from my girlfriend's snores and close my eyes.

Brown tiles coned over a crisscross of painted white bars. It's a round shrine. Around us black rails, thin. Shaded within the coned top as rains flood down, thick and angry.

"Your turn," I say and smile because I feel her at my back. She came after all.

Christmas dinner is serious in our house. Mom forces us into dress shirts and hands us platters of wine to pass around, like we're the help. Dad and I complain, but my girlfriend's a good sport. She's got a cute white dress on. A beige sweater on top. And flashes her perfect row of white teeth every chance she gets.

Dad of course slaps my back, proud. Mom too, but she's got all the cooking to do. Won't let us screw up a thing. Not since the disaster of 2009.

The last platter to go out is an eggnog, Baileys and whiskey mix Dad calls his special brew. I sigh and load up a pitcher and seven glasses to start. Walk out to where my pretty cousins stand around in sequins, their festive gold and silvers, highlights and perms fresh.

The doorbell goes off and platter in hand I go.

And of course it's her on the other side. Dark, dark eyes, and brown skin glowing in the front lights. Black lace of her collar wraps up around her long neck. Leaves her curved arms bare. Wrapped tight around her pinched waist, spreads and cuts off mid-thigh.

She seems grand and yet, feels small in my one-armed hug.

I follow her to the living room. Watch everyone become beige, their glitters fading, blurring to the edges of her spotlight.

My girlfriend is next to me, her words dull. I gesture with my free arm between them, introducing them. The girls exchange smiles, a beat of thick black lashes and my girlfriend steps past me, drawn to her nectar-sweet scent.

I watch those perfect brushstroke fingers wrap around my girlfriend's wrist and, for the briefest second, I'm apologetic for the ruin I've caused.

Soon she's gone. And my girlfriend becomes yet another flower torn and blown away in her wake.

But I'm not sorry long. I asked her to come.

My fiancé pops off the cork and moves over to the stove, emptying half the bottle into the pot. French cooking is her passion. And I'm the spectator. Waiting at the counter of our tiny shoebox condo for my treat.

"We'll get a bigger place," I promise, flashing my teeth, because today I got my first bonus. Not yet enough to bank in on my promise, but it's a start.

She pulls her auburn curls up and ties off a knot. "I like it here." She says it so often, I'm starting to believe her.

We eat then. It's good, always good. Though never as good as it smells when she brews, stirring all dreamlike over the pot.

In sync we wash up, brush, shower. Get into bed naked to tangle and lax. I feel her breathes slow, easing into the feather pillows, asleep. I want to follow her, but hard as I try, my mind is stone sober. Up.

And it's only when I close my eyes that I hear her call.

Back under the brown tiles, the coned top. Rain pouring outside, and safe in the shrine.

Her arms circle my waist from behind, her small face pressing lovingly into my back. Muffled, she murmurs, "I'm tired."

She says it over and over. But when she lets go, I force her to retreat, all the way to the far rails, until they dig into the back.

Her small chin fits between my index and thumb. Forced her face up to stare at me with her brown eyes wide.

"I'm not tired," I say.

"Okay." I blink, taken by surprise. She used to demand to get her way. Destroy and kill if she had to. But she smiles now, lopsided. Lashes beating low. Her fine fingers wrap around my palm. "I'll wait."

Four years and the bonuses pile, yet it's never enough. Me and my wife go from a shoebox to a closet in the grey hillside. A fetus to a screaming child. And the French recipes are gone.

Friday eve I stare around at the fluorescent tortoise shell my life's become. Three hundred unanswered emails. Texts I never bothered to check. And my phone buzzes, endlessly. Text after text from my wife.

I drop my head into my arms and, in the harsh glare of my computer screen, feel the pointless stretch ahead.

It's time.

I kiss my wife goodnight after the perfect Sunday. A late brunch: my specialty kimchi omelet for her, peanut butter pancakes for the toddler. Grandma babysat, let us have our first late night dinner in months. Her beef bourguignon. A wine bottle I got that was just slightly out of our price range. Coffee on the terrace. And later, she put on the red lingerie I got her for our forth anniversary, the last time we sent the toddler away.

Now she sleeps, rolled up in our sheets, sweaty, well fed.

Brushing away a stray fringe, I kiss her damp forehead and whisper, "Goodbye."

I leave her there.

My feet are bare on the ice-cold cement. The cone ceiling wards us from the rain, and yet, the wintery chill whips in and curls.

Her arm slinks around mine, binding us. Her warmth spreading through me from the caress of her skin against mine and all the way to my lips and toes. I taste her familiar scent on my tongue and swallow, nervous.

The first steps out are the hardest. Rain pours, ice cold on my face and arms. Running down my neck and inside my shirt. But I have her by me. Her warm, curves press closer as our clothes cling together, her breasts pressing harder against my arm with every breath. And that's when I know I'm okay.

The jitters don't go away though. Not as we walk the long way to the edge. And finally, we stand over at the brink, muddy feet, hair pressed to the sides of our face. Her lips are cold. Her tongue though, hot. One taste and I can't stop. Kiss her, kiss her, kiss her. Her long, perfect arms tighten around my neck, swaying on the spot 'til I lift her up. Her legs hitched up to my hips, locked.

This is exactly where we belong.

Holding her to me, lip to lip, noses bumping in our rush, she nudges me farther to where the cliff ends and the valley under is far.

Her weight tilts, ready, and I push off, tossing us over. Together we fall.

SAFE HAVEN

Samuel Agro

This far into the wastelands of the northern provinces, the freezing winds blasted frigid air into every tiny crack and seam of Ambra's winter gear. Her long trek-- six days into the northern regions-- was nearing its end. She'd left behind the final outpost of Balhar province, and the last warm bed, nearly two days before. She'd kept up a steady pace since then, knowing that to stop in this arctic cold was to acquiesce to death.

But she would not die today. Her receiver, tucked away inside her coats close to her heart, had begun to ping quietly in response to the beacon an hour ago, and even now it's frequency had increased, letting her know she was within yards of her goal.

She struggled upward through the deep, hard-packed snow of the enormous drift before her, and skidded down the other side into a low valley, where the wind had swept the ground nearly clear, revealing patches of the hard, lifeless soil of the flatlands. Ambra's receiver shifted from a ping to a long continuous tone, and she felt the ground begin to vibrate under her heavy boots. About twenty feet ahead she saw the access tube rising from the ground, shaking off clumps of frozen snow as it thrust upward. It stopped and stood, a slender cylinder of gray in the blanket of white. As Ambra moved toward it the doors opened automatically, and after she entered the small elevator carriage they closed behind her. Her stomach flipped as the carriage sped downward into the hallowed halls of the Cathedral.

The car slowed gently to a stop and the doors opened, revealing a long, curving, mostly featureless hallway, constructed of blue polymer panels. Ambra loosened the collar of her coat in welcome response to the geothermic heat of the underground structure. She shifted her heavy pack from her shoulders to her right hand and proceeded down the hallway. In about twenty meters she encountered another doorway, which opened as she neared it, making it unnecessary to break her stride. In another instant she was in the fabled Core Compartment of the Cathedral. The room was nearly a hundred meters across and sixty high, with two mezzanines full of unfamiliar machines and technologies, encircling the room. High above a skylight seemed, miraculously, to beam sunlight into the room, though Ambra knew they were a kilometer or more below the surface of the planet.

She was welcomed by three of The Devout, dressed in their simple gray robes and wearing white ceremonial skullcaps on their shaven heads. The garb left little to differentiate their sex or social standing. Two of The Devout relieved her of her pack and coat, while the third-- probably the Abbot-- stepped up to her and appraised her with a cynical eye.

After a moment she spoke.

"Are you a willing vessel?"

"I am," declared Ambra, trying to sound more confident than she felt.

"By the Book," the Abbot responded. "First we shall proceed with the implantation, then you may eat and take rest."

The Abbot led her up a long staircase to the first mezzanine. Here were many sacred devices, set into the walls and floor, blue and red lights blinking softly in the rarefied atmosphere of the Core Compartment. The technology of The Devout, so far beyond that of the outer world, seemed almost like magic. Another disciple awaited them there, standing near a porcelain table. The table was inset with small glowing screens, and an opening where one would naturally lay their head. The technician cleansed Ambra's scalp and neck with a strong-smelling liquid and dried her with a soft, absorbent cloth. The disciple instructed her to lie down on the table. As she reclined restraints encircled her head, holding her in place. The technician depressed a key on one of the glowing screens. With a low hum, and a sudden electrical snap, the chip was implanted into the base of her skull.

A tingling then, as the technological tendrils of the implant spread into her brain, entangling with ganglia and merging with synapses. It didn't hurt, exactly, but there was a strange sensation. A gradual blossoming of space inside her mind, as though a cottage had become a manor house. After a few moments the tingling ceased and the restraints slid away. The Abbot and the technician helped her to her feet and they all descended from the mezzanine.

"By the Book," said the Abbot.

"By the Book," Ambra replied, and the Abbot took her leave.

The others returned her belongings to her and led her into another curving hallway, in which were set the doors to many small cells. Inside them awaited other Vessels, she knew, but she saw no one. Her room was small, but warm, and more inviting than the stark vastness of the Core Compartment. Inside she found food, drink and a comfortable bed. She ate, drank, eliminated with great relief in the attached privy, and collapsed into a torpid slumber. She dreamed of vast empty spaces in her mind. Her consciousness seemed a dark, hollow vacuum, crying out to be filled.

A delicate chime teased her into wakefulness. Ambra rose, showered, and donned a shapeless saffron shift that hung in a small alcove near her gear. Another chime, louder and more solemn, called her to The Ceremony. She exited her room into the hallway and joined the other Vessels, similarly clad, similarly excited and apprehensive. They fell into an easy lockstep and traversed the long hall into the Cathedral. If the Core Compartment was impressive, this chamber was awe-inspiring. It was easily thrice as large, and was the only room she'd seen that favoured aesthetic over functionality. It was a triumph of spiritual architecture featuring huge, glowing windows, soaring spires and ornate filigree.

The Vessels, eleven in all, convened in a semi-circle in front of several technological pods. They stood, facing outwards into the Cathedral. A grim-faced procession of The Devout entered, chanting a low catechism. Behind them followed The Supplicants, Cordollans all, outcasts from the nearby planet Cordalon. They were a tall, willowy race, their flesh a mottled green and yellow. Their faces were unsettling, with mouths too low, and noses too high, and with four ocular sense organs, recessed and purplish, two on either side of the nose, and two on the sloping sides of their ample foreheads. They had no hair to speak of. Their breathing apparatuses were secured over their mouths and noses, but even with these it was clear the Cordollans were suffering in our inhospitable atmosphere. They all wore the pale blue robes of The Supplicant. They each stood before their Vessel, and bowed low in respect and gratitude.

The Abbott stepped forward.

"Vessels, it is not too late to forgo this ritual. If you are no longer committed, you may leave now and none shall shame you. Only the willing may take this final step."

There was a long pause. Ambra steeled herself, and no Vessel reneged.

"Very well. From this moment you are all obligated," the Abbot intoned. "By the Book."

"By the book," they answered.

Many of The Devout came forward then, attaching leads from the pods to the implants of the Supplicants and their Vessels. Gentle electrical impulses lulled them into sleep and the transference began. The new, empty compartments of Ambra's mind began to fill with the thoughts and memories of her Supplicant, B'al Totht. Flashes of the war and strife of Cordolla flooded into her brain. The angry red and blue faces of the oppressors as they drove the green and yellow race before them. She saw how they enslaved and abused them, murdered and desecrated them. She experienced it as the family and friends of The Supplicants were incarcerated, beaten, and slain. She saw as they made a desperate escape from their forsaken planet in stolen space ships.

Then came a wave of gratitude for her sacrifice, and for the home she was making inside her mind for B'al Totht. They communed for a time, their minds mingling, merging, all his memories becoming hers, and hers his. Two, yet not two. One, yet not one.

Ambra awoke.

Next to her B'al Totht's body slumped, an empty shell. The bodies of the Cordollans could not survive in the atmosphere of her planet, and nor could they live under the tyranny of their own. They had appealed to The Devout, with their advanced technology and enlightened creed, and had been offered this solution: Sanctuary in the minds of the Vessels until such time as they might find justice on their own planet.

B'al would exist as part of her, thus given succor and new life until he might one day be free of his subjugation and be transferred into the mind of one of their own race. Their essential selves would go on, sharing the lives and experiences of their hosts. It was a great giving. It was A Holy Thing.

Ambra's heart sang with joy, and B'al's heart sang back, in perfect harmony.

Author's Note

All in all, I was pretty happy with how the story turned out. I told the tale I wanted to tell, though it feels a little compressed at the moment, and has a little more exposition that I would prefer. I might expand the story at a later date, give it some breathing room and smooth over the phrasing. But, I think it reads pretty well for something that was completed in less than 10 hours.

BITTER SHORES

Katie Vane

Eilsa didn't believe me at first, despite the fish churning upside down in the surf above us, despite the dark red sores blooming across her fur. Not until our sisters' bodies started washing ashore.

She stands for the first time on unsteady legs, naked, the water still lapping at her calves. Her pelt, beautiful mottled grey, hangs limp in her bony arms. Her eyes, brilliant green now, are unfocused. She stares up at the pebbled beach. She consented to this deal I've made, but now that she is here, she is unable to take another step.

All around us, our sisters stagger from the sea, staring in abjection at the pelts in their arms. They look back, every one of them, yearning as I do to dive back into the sea foam. But the sulfur burning through their nostrils and the bodies littering the shoreline remind them why they're here. Better to step breathing onto the beach than to let the waves roll our bodies ashore. The men here will share their islands and their beds with us, and my sisters will survive.

I step forward and take Eilsa's spindly hands—something I could never have done under the sea—and guide her to dry land.

"See," I say, nodding to my skin folded neatly on a jut of stone nearby. "Just like this…"

Her arms fall limp to her sides as I fold her pelt for her and lay it next to mine. She shivers and curls her body inwards, sensing just as I do that there is something shameful, now, about having our bodies open to the world.

I step close and drape my arm across her waist, touch my forehead to hers. "The men will be here soon," I say.

"The wind," she says, and shivers again as a gust blows down from the rocky cliffs and through us all.

I feel the bumps raising on her new skin.

"Look," I say as the first man appears on the horizon, staring down at us from the edge of the village. I raise an arm, haltingly, in greeting. I must set an example for my sisters.

The man starts down the rocky hill and more follow, one for each of us.

A low murmur starts on the beach, my sisters afraid, asking each other what happens now. I turn to them and make the voice in this strange smooth throat as strong as I can. "The sea is death now," I say. My sisters look at me with bewilderment and with hate. "This is how we carry on."

The first man reaches the beach and approaches me, his dark brown eyes fixed on mine. I stifle a trill of fear and reach for my skin. It feels cool beneath my fingers.

The man stops near enough to touch and lowers his eyes, murmurs something in a language I will never understand. I offer him my pelt, and he takes it reverently. In return, he drapes a scratchy blanket over my shoulders that irritates my soft skin. He gently takes my hand in his rough, weathered fingers. I know to call him Declan and he knows to call me Aoire, but that is where our knowledge of each other ends.

I turn to face my sisters, hand in hand with this man.

My sisters hang back, some clutching their pelts to their chests, many shaking visibly. But they are all silent now, not a wail or a whisper to be heard. If they will be leaving the sea this night, they will at least be listening to its parting call.

One of the men approaches Eilsa, his eyes low on her body, and anger rumbles deep in my throat like the roar of plunging currents. I feel a gentle tug on my hand and realize I've taken a step forward, towards her. Declan is holding me back, keeping me by his side.

The other man kneels before Eilsa, and I see his lips move in the moonlight. Eilsa, confused, finds my eyes. I push back my shoulders and nod. She offers the man her pelt and he takes it, then her hand. I think I am going to retch.

This is how my sisters survive.

A few years pass, each of us in our own homes with our own husbands. We prepare meals, sweep floors, and bear children. Declan's speech is foreign but gentle, as is his touch. I make myself search out comfort in his arms and, later, in the arms of our children.

It helps a little, but only sometimes. On those rare days when the ocean salt is strong enough in the air to drown out the sulfur, there is nothing to be done for me.

I keep my sisters' pelts all locked away inside a heavy iron chest, collected from the husbands so I can keep them safe. Four years have passed when I find it gaping wide, my intricate lock somehow tricked open.

The first pelt has gone missing.

Two days later, Ora washes ashore. Her sleek grey body lies limp next to the corpses of the small creatures, fish and crabs and birds, with whom we once shared a home.

Seven months later, a second pelt disappears, despite my best efforts to keep the chest secure. Chira. A little more time passes and then it's Dheni, then Maiha, Eruwe, Osimi. The sea always rolls their bodies back to us, speckled pelts marred with open red sores, round black eyes staring dead into the sky.

I want the men to move the bodies before the bugs set in, but they're afraid of us like this, and angry besides. They leave us on the beach to rot.

I do what I can to safeguard the chest, but every effort is circumvented. There is no keeping my sisters out. Always they find a way in.

Declan wants me to burn the chest.

I cannot.

In the ninth year, Eilsa's pelt goes missing.

I scramble to the beach with my feeble heart thudding behind my ribs. My sister is there, standing naked on the beach on her two thin, bleached-coral legs, staring out at the ocean. Each vertebrae casts its own shadow across her sallow skin. A rush of relief threatens to collapse me.

"Teis's body never came ashore," Eilsa murmurs. "It's been nearly three weeks."

My mouth is dry. "So she lies still on the ocean floor."

"Or she swims free." Eilsa half-turns her head toward me, her profile stark in the moonlight. "Do you not feel it, Aoire? All these years, has it not been calling to you?"

Of course it has. I hear the whistling of the dolphins in my dreams, taste the blood of an otter after a long hunt. I long to chatter and to dive, to soar as the songs of the great whales echo in the waters around me.

"Look down," I say, my voice stiff. I must convince her. "Every tide washes more fish onto this beach. The sea has not stopped killing us."

"These fish are small. Teis is stronger. Perhaps our sisters can survive it now."

No. The sea is death.

"Think of Iollan. Your son, bound to this rock. Would you go where he cannot follow?" I conjure in my mind the faces of my own red-haired daughters as the swell of the waves laps against my resolve. "Is there not enough on this rock to love?" My voice breaks. "Would you leave me here, Eilsa, without my sister?"

She is quiet for a time, and my pulse races.

"You were right to bring us here, Aoire, but that time has passed. We try again for the sea or we shrivel on the shore."

The wind rushes past my ears and scalds my cheeks with specks of sand. I have tried so hard to keep my sisters safe, and one by one they have abandoned me. Tonight, on this beach, I smell salt, not sulfur. I ache to feel the ocean swell.

Tomorrow I will burn the chest.

Eilsa turns. In her arms she carries not one pelt, but two. She offers mine to me, a silky gray that shines in the moonlight.

I take it numbly. Her pelt shimmers as she drapes it over her shoulders and pulls it closed around her.

Then she steps into the sea, and I am afraid I might follow. To swim with her one last time, just a taste, a memory that will last me the rest of my days on land.

I leave my clothes folded neatly on a jut of stone nearby. I slip into my sealskin with a shudder and a sigh. The living pelt clings to every curve, smoothing me over, reminding me I am sleek and vibrant and of the sea. My sisters are calling to me, chirping and hooting, lost to me forever.

I stop just short of the ocean and wait for the water to come to me. Finally, a small, salty wave crawls near enough to douse my moonlit toes. My entire body convulses and I cannot tell which is stronger, the panic or the desire. My body dives and the water closes over my head.

Welcome home, it whispers.

IN THE ZONE

Brandon Butler

Amy watched across the street as the Constants in their fine black, white and blue uniforms surrounded the boy as he stared into his phone. Three of them, one of him. Belts and shoulder-pads versus a t-shirt and slacks. They didn't move for their weapons but wore them openly at their sides, ready for use. Two stood by each of his shoulders as the middle one came up and said something. The young man nodded. He was maybe sixteen or seventeen but didn't look the sort to put up a fight. As a group they walked him from the concrete rim of the open air fountain to the hovervan waiting across the street. Quietly under the noise of a busy afternoon, they hustled him into the back seat and sped away.

"Poor kid," said Lyanna, sitting back in her restaurant patio chair. She took a big sip on her long island iced tea and sat back. "Another victim of the hallowed update schedule."

"That wasn't about the updates," Amy said. She shook her head. "You always say that. It could have been anything."

Lyanna shrugged. "I'm telling you it was the update. You could see it on his face."

Amy rolled her eyes and brought out her own phone. She called up appZone because with all this talking about it, it didn't hurt to make sure something had happened since last night. The splash screen came up in the cartoony red lettering with lightning bolts stabbing out from either end of the 'Z'. Yeah, real original branding, guys. But Amy still had to stifle her sigh of relief when the version number came out all clear as the most current before the app auto-toggled to its main screen showing her position and name on a local map within her bright customized pink and blue overlay, its popups traced in curling frames of gold: *Amy Furlong, 23, Albanz Restaurant, Section 34*. She pocketed the phone and noticed Lyanna smiling over practically every inch of her smug face. "Worried, were we?" she asked.

"Shut up."

"Hey, I wish it wasn't so necessary either," Lyanna said. "But the Zone's a precious sort of place. Everyone wants in and they have to keep track of everyone that needs keeping track of. And if they can't keep track of you…" she gave a little shrug. "What's the point?"

Amy shook her head. She looked around at the people calmly passing by as if nothing had happened, shopping and talking and making the very best of an average sunny day in the comfort and stability of the Zone. "You know it's not as fair as all that," she said. "You and I, we're born in-Zone. But the ones they let in, the offsiders? Do they even know the rules? Wasn't it you who told me most offsiders don't make it through their first month?"

"Probably. That's the price of order. Look, we all get the app. If you fall off the update wagon, that's on you."

"Uh-huh."

"I'm serious." Lyanna forward again, strands of her long hair hanging like red vines over her lap. Amy knew they'd wandered into one of her favorite sorts of subjects and she wouldn't just let it go like a nice, sensible person. "Do you know what it was like before? Remember? I did that proj-"

"-Project back in first year Ethics. Yes I *know*, Lyanna. By now, everyone knows."

But Lyanna talked on, unfazed. "It was all chaos back then. No standards, only a handful of protocols worth a damn. Even email programs had all these lopsided rendering engines that radically changed from version to version and nobody could agree on anything. It took a while for us to adopt the *correct* Operating System. The *established* Virtual Reality engine. The proper way to live like decent, professional human beings. Software programmed the way it's supposed to and social media flowing through all the proper channels. Otherwise it's just..." she bent her head low, searching for the words. "...nonsense. What's the point of the Zone if you're just going to let people do what they want and put it out for people to use? No standards whatsoever."

Amy patted her hand. Lyanna could get fired up when talking about this stuff, but then it was an easy thing to get fired up about, these days. "I get it, love, I do. I just think it's unfair managing it like this. I mean, one missed update for too long and you're out the door?"

"If you saw the lines of the people trying to get in, you'd understand."

"Well..." Amy sighed, then drained the last of her iced tea, a twin to Lyanna's own. "Understanding was never my strong suit."

They said their goodbyes maybe an hour later and Amy went home, taking transit all the way uptown. She thought for the first time in a while about the smoothness of the ride, how a seat always seemed to be available and how punctual everything ran. Subway precisely arriving at quarter past six, leaving exactly 15 seconds later. Line up, get on one after the other or wait for the next. No pushing or shoving please or you'd have the Constants come and sort you out. Had it really not been always like this? What kind of a place had that been, and how had it stayed together? If Lyanna was right, it hurt your head just thinking about it.

Still, they could be a little more forgiving with these update expectations, acting as if everyone would get them at the same time. Sometimes people had to head into out of service areas or go underground or sometimes maintenance was going on and it you really had to fight to prove those edge cases. You had only so many hours, maybe half a day to finish the whole cycle and if you missed it, that was it. You were out. The Zone had its share of hardasses calling the shots, that was for sure.

She went home and took in a couple hours of polite streaming over her wide-screen smart tv. The iced teas had put her in the mood for more so she made a couple at home, spiking them with a few extra touches of whiskey. Amy usually had this casual, arms-length relationship with alcohol and usually knew when to pull back. But today had been one of those days where not much happens other than watching some sad little average kid get swooped up by the Constants and their iconic hovervan. She could still see that horrified look over his acne-potted face. A little more juice from the bottle couldn't hurt.

When she woke up, it was noon the next day. Had she slept all that time? Jesus. She got up, took a shower, and was walking around in her robe when she picked up her phone and opened the app.

UPDATE WARNING: MISSED UPLOAD A734HJ6 at 2 a.m. EST. APPROVE UPDATE VERSION IMMEDIATELY.

Oh shit. Oh shit, oh shit, oh shit.

She flipped over to the settings tab and approved the queued update. Why did she have to approve this, did anyone ever *not* approve an update? She paced across the apartment as the download began. This was bullcrap. They make a release at two in the morning and expect you to be right on board in the middle of the night? Who does that? If appZone had any sort of customer service line or email address or anything she'd call the number right here and now and let them have it but… well, that had never been a thing with appZone. Citizens heard from them and not the other way around.

She looked out her window at to the street below. It was empty. A few messages from her parents and Lyanna were on her phone from last night warning her about the after hours update, but it looked like she'd somehow pocket-changed the settings to vibrate instead of chime. Goddamn touchy touchscreens.

The blue bar crept along left to right in the center of her screen. Ten percent. Fifteen percent. Twenty-five.

Come on, come on…

Somewhere around eighty percent there was a knock at her door. Miss Dorhees from down the hall, wanting to borrow a cup of sugar. Miss Dorhees was pretty much right up skirting the edge of dementia and had apparently forgot she'd asked for the same thing two nights ago, and who still asks for cups of sugar when you can get it ordered to your front door. It was, like, generations ago that had been a thing, and it wasn't even her generation. If it wasn't for her grown kids taking care of everything – except this, apparently – she'd have been removed from the Zone long ago. But Amy gave her the cup of whatever and got the old bat off her doorstep.

She went to her phone. *Update downloaded.* It had probably had been sitting there a whole entire minute. Amy installed the update as quick as her fumbling fingers could press the button.

An hour later, it all seemed good. The update was downloaded and installed, everything looked about right. Cripes. She made a silent deal with herself never to do *that* again, whatever it was that had gotten her into this jam. Living in the shadow of appZone had become its own game of survival and every year seemed a little harder to survive.

What a morning. She got dressed and put on her jacket and went for a long walk.

The Constants converged on her about twenty minutes outside her door. "Please come with us, ma'am," one said. He sounded the sort that wasn't going to mess around.

She'd never really interacted with one before. Not once in her life. "What's this about?"

He just said, "Please come with us ma'am."

She tried a smile. She knew it must look nervous and weak crawling across her flushed face but a good smile was worth a hundred casual hellos, right? "Is this about appZone? The update? I know… I mean… hey, what's up with that late night update, am I right?"

They didn't react. They didn't cuff her over the head and drag her away but they didn't smile back, either.

"Hey, I don't know what new schedule they've got us on, but look." Amy opened up her phone, called up appZone, showed them the familiar splash screen with its current version number. "I got the update, it's installed! Look! Right here!"

The head Constant held out his hand and she felt herself relax as she handed over her phone. Close call, but she'd sorted in in time. They were never making her leave this wonderful place. The Zone, where everything was expected, comfortable and anything complicated just went away without complaint. No unwanted surprises besides the occasional batty neighbor at your door who they were probably dragging off any day now, no challenge in your way that you'd ever possibly fail. The Zone now, the Zone forever. Never take me from this haven, my refuge of ceaseless safety, my proud and stable home.

"It's not activated," the head Constant said.

"What's that?"

"Your update. You installed it, but you didn't activate it. New feature, see?" He held up Amy's phone to her face so she could see the glowing green button in the center of the screen. Then he touched it and the interface on the app changed, ever so slightly. One of the buttons that had been hugging the left side of the screen swapped itself over to the right. Amy seemed to remember it being back there originally, four or five versions ago. It was the only thing that looked any different.

"Please come with us, ma'am," the head Constant said again.

Amy took a deep breath, then broke into a run.

She only got a short distance before she felt a shock along her back. Everything went numb as she fell to the ground, the blades of a healthy, perfectly manicured lawn pressed against her face. She could smell the grass. She closed her eyes and tried forcing her brain to remember the scent. It might be a long time before she'd walk over earth this green again.

Then the Constants grabbed her by the shoulders and lifted her from the ground.

The next hours were a blur. Her memory was getting fuzzy. She remembered a bench, a courtroom, people talking to her, but she only half-understood what they said. Something about being in breach of appZone. Her sanctuary citizenship was summarily revoked. She could re-apply like anyone else in another year, but

Amy and everything she owned were to be removed from the Zone. Immediately.

The sentence had been handed down but Amy kept pleading her case. Tears mixed with black mascara ran down her cheeks like oily rain as she asked them for another look. She'd never received any sort of infraction for anything, ever. She tried really hard to follow the rules, all of them, even the stupid ones she'd always hated. This wasn't fair. She was a good girl.

The powers that be nodded. They had sympathetic eyes but mouths that remained shut hard and tight. Something in Amy wondered how often they had seen others like her, how often they'd heard these pleas.

And then the thought struck her that even if she proved her innocence, she'd still lose.

She remembered surrendering with a whimper as she looked down at her phone. AppZone was gone from the list of icons, uninstalled against her will.

One of the Constants by the courthouse door watched her as she passed by, stopping for a moment to leaning against the wall. "Don't take it personal," she recalled him saying. "People in, people out. Keeps everyone happy. It's only fair."

Amy looked at him a long moment. Her stare seemed to make him uncomfortable. Her hair must have been one frizzy, jumbled up terror of a mess. "You ever been where I'm going?" she asked him.

"What, me? Outside the Zone? Oh, *hell* no."

It was maybe another day when they escorted her to the main gate. Carrying only her suitcase, she was with a bunch of others, nobody she'd ever met, everyone looking as dejected and morose as she. Probably none of them had bothered bathing or changing. The Constants driving the truck – an old-timey truck, it didn't hover or anything -- took them straight to the border then let them out the back to a new world of overcast skies, leafless trees and beige-looking people that passed by with an occasional glance.

Amy got down. She watched the others wander off to whatever fate awaited them. The Constants got back in their truck and drove away without a goodbye. She walked a short distance, then came up to someone standing by the dirt road that hadn't been on the truck with her. "Hi," she said.

"Hi," he said back. His face was pretty grimy.

"You live here?"

He nodded.

"What's it like?"

The man looked off in the direction of the departing truck. "You from the Zone?"

It was Amy's turn to nod.

"It's not so bad. Not so nice as in the Zone, though."

Oh. Not so bad. Ok, ok… "You ever been to the Zone?" Amy asked him.

"No," he said, "but I know others that been. They got some tall tales."

"What's the biggest difference, from what you've heard?"

"Oh that's easy," he said. "No wi-fi."

Amy fell to her knees. Jesus Christ. It would have been kinder if they'd just shot her.

GLASS HEART GIANT

Y.M. Pang

We lived in the glass heart of a giant. For many sleeptimes now, we've tried to escape.

We woke in spun-glass cocoons, naked, and rolled out to find a stack of glass plates and folded clothes. We strode on pockmarked glass, to rivers flowing red with the giant's blood. We found each other, the seven of us, as we wandered the pulsating chambers. The thump-thump of the giant's heart was a constant around us, until we wondered what silence was and why the word was in our vocabulary.

In those early days we slept in our cocoons, and ate succulent red fruit from sparkling glass trees. Our hands and lips grew bloody red, though the fruit was sweet, not salt and metal like the giant's blood. Sometimes Sigfir and I made love on the smooth glass of the riverbanks, or in my spun-glass cocoon.

Isaba spent her days pacing near the mitral valve, singing. Maiya stayed in the glass orchards long past mealtimes, running through exercises that could've been dance or battle preparation. Zulin, always silent, disappeared for long periods of time. Once we crawled to the left ventricle, where his dwelling was located, to check on him, just to make sure he was still alive. We found his cocoon empty, but three sleeptimes later, he returned to the orchards, gaunt and silent but breathing. Erjawu and Roman,

110

inseparable, often leapt into the gushing river just for the thrill of being sent thundering downstream, until they hit a valve that spat them out and back onto glassy ground. They mused about making "dishes" with the red fruits, except we had no knives or pots, and the fruits simply turned into more red mush on their olive-skinned hands.

All of us had glass plates in our dwellings, a thick pile of them, which I called our library. After those first hedonistic times of eating and sleeping and lovemaking had passed, I began combing through them, obsessing over the plates every moment when Sigfir and I were not obsessing over each other. There seemed no pattern nor commonality between the plates. Some showed tall, thin structures I knew were called towers. Some had colourful characters with bubbles popping from their mouths, little squiggles in those bubbles. I didn't know what those squiggles were, until I showed that plate to Erjawu. He said they were words, and read them to me, except they were nonsensical things about escaping criminals and uncomfortable capes which meant nothing in the context of our lives. One glass plate had nothing but black squiggles.

Sigfir was the first to desire escape. He climbed through the chambers of the giant's heart, ran his hands across glass walls, pressed his ear to pulsating riverbanks. He dipped his finger into the river and drew in scarlet on the banks: maps and diagrams of the heart that encased us. He once carved—with his fingernails—his approximation of the heart's shape on one of the bigger fruits. It had two curves on the top, and tapered to a point at the bottom. I loved watching him work, his strong, golden-skinned hands deft and precise with every label.

He gathered all of us together, even the reticent Zulin. He said, "We have to get out."

We agreed, because by then we no longer had unthinking minds. We'd taken to wearing the clothes laid out for us. We had each developed our own rituals, personalities.

But glass could be surprisingly hard to break without metal, without the swords Maiya reminisced about. We slammed our fists against the outer walls of the heart. We threw our plates at it, and managed to scratch neither plate nor wall. Maiya snapped off the branches of the delicate trees and tried to cut the heart with it, but the branches shattered as expected.

Over many sleeptimes we did this. We beat our fists bloody. Two of the trees withered and died, and Sigfir asked Maiya to stop lest we lose our food supply. Some of us barely remembered to eat. I wondered if we were deteriorating, reverting to our single-minded state at awakening, when we knew nothing but sleep and food and sex.

I wandered to the middle of the heart. There was a strange device here, a mass of tubes and slots, shaped suspiciously like that strange fruit sculpture Sigfir had made. My mind flashed back to the glass plates. Then to something *before* the glass plates and the giant's heart and waking up inside that shining cocoon. Pump, motor... Perhaps this was the heart's motor. If we could stop it...

I kicked it. I gripped the tubes and pulled. I found one of Maiya's flimsy tree-branch swords and hacked at it. The heartbeat around me thundered on.

By now the others had crowded around the device. Sigfir and Maiya joined me in my attack. Zulin paced around the device, frowning. "Something doesn't belong," he said.

Sigfir and I stopped, looking at him in puzzlement. Maiya aimed another vicious kick.

Ducking her foot, Zulin knelt and gripped one part of the device: a black box about the size of two human feet. Now that he mentioned it, the box stuck out. It broke the shape that otherwise resembled Sigfir's approximation of the giant's heart. Zulin pulled it free, turned it in his hands. On the side of the box was a silver rectangle decorated with buttons. A keypad, I knew instinctively.

"We have to find the key," Sigfir said.

Erjawu disagreed. "Let's just input numbers until we find one that opens it. After all, we've got nothing but time."

We did this for a while, taking turns, keeping track of which number we'd gotten up to by scribbling with blood on the riverbanks. The task was complicated by how we didn't even know the number of digits in the passcode.

I thought back to the glass plates. There must be a clue within. "I'm going to take a look," I told the others.

"Juno…" Erjawu said.

"If you wish to keep trying higher numbers, you can do that in the meantime."

I went back to my dwelling. All of the others' plates were already there; I was the only one still interested in analyzing them, so they'd given theirs to me.

I spread the plates out on the floor. Sigfir had come with me. He swept back his brown hair, stared at the plates with intense eyes. Some animal part of me desired him, right then, right there, but that must be what the giant wanted, to keep us thoughtless and dreaming. We'd been like that for too long.

Each of the others had a plate similar to one of mine: a mostly clear plate with squiggles, though for every one the ink blots were in different places. I laid the seven plates over each other, and it became a splotchy mess of black ink. But… I frowned. There was something here.

I paired the plates. Mine over Sigfir's. Erjawu's over Roman's. Maiya and Isaba and Zulin together. It took a few tries to find the right combinations, but in the end they shaped numbers.

"Incredible," Sigfir said.

I shook my head. "But in what order?"

He clapped me on the shoulder. "You'll figure it out."

I did. I ran my hands down the corners of the plates, and felt carvings on mine, Erjawu's, and Maiya's. My hands weren't sensitive enough to figure out what numbers they traced, but Sigfir's were. "That must be our order," he said.

"Let's get back," I said.

I sprinted back to the centre of the heart and laid out the plates. Isaba gasped, and even Maiya and Zulin looked impressed.

"Numbers," Enjawu muttered. "Doesn't mean they're the right ones."

"What else could they be?" I grabbed the box and punched the numbers into the keypad. I prayed it would work, though I've never known any god except the giant.

The black box clicked open.

I lifted the lid, carefully, reverently. And music poured out.

A simple melody, played by a single instrument. Several of us rose to our feet, as if trying to locate a greater source, but the sound came from the open black box.

Within it was a figurine, much more detailed than anything Sigfir had carved. A slender girl in a puffed dress stood on her tiptoes, her other leg extended behind her, her brown hair knotted into a bun. She spun around and around as the music played. Her painted eyes seemed sharp, alive.

I dropped the lid, closing the box. The music cut off.

"Now what?" Erjawu said. "We opened a box and a song started playing?"

The *thump-thump* of the giant's heart thundered around us, almost mocking.

"Open it again," Isaba said.

I obeyed. The song began to play, from the beginning. The dancer spun around and around.

"Those strings…" Isaba said.

"Strings?" Sigfir and I said together. He, too, stared at the dancer.

"Not the ballerina. The harpist."

I didn't know what was a ballerina or a harpist, though the words sounded familiar. But I looked to the side of the box, and found another figure there. Another woman, this one sitting, immobile. On the black velvet beside her was a strangely shaped wooden frame lined with strings, on which the woman's hands rested.

"Heartstrings," Isaba whispered. She leapt to her feet, and ran.

"Hey!" I called, sprinting after her. "Tell us what's going on. Don't just run off!"

We followed her. She climbed, then headed across the latticework tunnel, toward the mitral valve. The valve opened and blood spilled through, then it closed again to the sound of the giant's heartbeat. Chordae tendineae tugged on the opening, controlling it, their colour milky white against the clear glass.

"Where's the music box?" Isaba said.

I looked down. I'd left it behind when I went to chase her.

"Here," Sigfir said, holding it out. As always, he'd thought things through. He hadn't let momentary excitement lead him from the goal.

"Play it," Isaba said.

Sigfir opened the box. Isaba stood and listened, hushing anyone who spoke. She listened until the song finished, as it started from the beginning once again.

Isaba reached out, grabbed one of the beams, and climbed onto the latticework. From there she could just about reach the chordae tendineae. She brushed a hand across one, which sang out a single note.

Balanced on the latticework, Isaba strummed different chordae. "They're in the wrong order," she muttered, and the rest of us looked at each other in confusion, not sure what order they were supposed to be in or how they were wrong. I did notice that every chorda had a different associated note.

After a few minutes of this, Isaba instructed Sigfir to open the box. She strummed some notes as the music played, whispering to herself, her voice barely audible beneath the music.

As the song repeated, she began playing along with it. She shuffled across the latticework, strumming cords. Erjawu spread his arms, as if to catch her if she fell, though I doubted he'd have the strength to grab a falling glass shard, let alone Isaba.

At the end of the song, Sigfir shut the box. "Can you play it?" he said, "There are only seven heartstrings here. What about the semitones?"

Semitones?

"No, this song doesn't have semitones," Isaba said.

"Maybe the semitones are on the tricuspid valve." From the quirk of his mouth, the spark in his eyes, I realized Sigfir was making a joke, though for once I couldn't understand what the joke was.

"Let's hope I don't have to use them," Isaba said.

I laid a hand on Sigfir's arm. "Sig, you know about music too?"

"No. Not really." He shook his head. "I just remembered something."

Isaba asked Sigfir to keep the box shut, and she played the entire song again, with the chordae only. It was impressive—watching her dance across the latticework reminded me of an image from the glass plates, of a woman walking over a blue river on a thin cord. I didn't know how Isaba had managed to memorize all the notes so quickly, and how she had the instinct to match them to the chordae.

But at the end of her song, nothing happened.

"Maybe I need to play it along with the music box," she said.

"Maybe you need to play it with the music box back in the motor," Sigfir said. "I took a look at it earlier. Zulin's right, it doesn't belong to the shape of a heart. But it does connect to something, which disconnected when we removed it."

Sigfir, Zulin, and I climbed down the latticework, back to the motor. Zulin fitted the box back to the heart. Sigfir opened the box and we all held our breaths as music began to play.

Above us, Isaba danced across the latticework, strumming. She looked like some combination of the dancer in the box and the figurine she'd called a harpist.

We felt it. Every time Isaba struck a note at the same as the box, the walls around us shuddered. I found Sigfir's hand; his grip was warm, but I felt freezing cold. I alternated between staring up at the lattice and Isaba, and staring at him, the gold of his skin, the soft brown of his hair.

It took Isaba a few tries. The third time, she matched the music box perfectly, each strum in sync with it. At the final note, the glass heart began to shake.

Zulin dove to the ground, covering his head with his arms. He was the smart one. Sigfir and I just stood there, staring, as the latticework collapsed. The shrieks of Isaba and the others punctuated the sound of shattering glass. Sigfir leapt forward, as if trying to catch someone—Isaba? Roman? I grabbed him and pinned him to the ground, covering his body with mine. In that moment I didn't care whether any of others would be hurt by the fall. I just wanted to protect Sigfir, everything else be damned.

Glass fell and shattered against me. I felt the slick of my own blood, but it wasn't painful, no more than Sigfir's nails on my back when we made love. I risked a glance up, just in time to see an entire section of heart wall crash beside the motor.

Then, silence. No, not silence. Just the usual thump-thump of the giant's heart. I tasted bile at the back of my throat. Had all that we'd done led nowhere?

Sigfir turned onto his back, so that we were face to face. His every feature was intimately familiar, from the turn of his nose to his long lashes. He reached out, brushing glass shards from my hair. "Juno," he said, "are you okay?"

I pushed myself off him and stood. "I'm fine."

"Why did you do that?"

"Why did you try to catch them?"

He fell silent, knowing our responses would be similar.

All around us the others stumbled to their feet. We were all cut, but none seriously. Isaba, Maiya, Roman, and Erjawu, the ones who'd fallen from the lattice, were bruised but hadn't broken any bones. Isaba had felt the glass become fleshy soft at the moment of landing, though the others dismissed this as her imagination.

We picked glass shards from each other's skin before going to the fallen piece of wall. We let out a collective groan when we drew close. For when Sigfir reached forward, his hand connected with another barrier.

Then we gasped. While before the heart's glass had been frosted, this portion was now clear, like the uncoloured parts of the plates. And through it we saw the pink-red layers of the giant's muscle, the white branches of her ribs.

"So close…" Isaba said. Zulin muttered something about endocardium and myocardium, and we all wondered if he was going crazy, or maybe he had remembered something.

Sigfir ran his hands across the clear wall. At a specific point, a bit below chest height, his hand stopped.

"Here," he said. "The last thing."

There was a slot in the glass. I traced it. It had two sweeping curves at the top, and tapered to a slight point on the bottom.

Sigfir drew a breath. "Well, at least we don't have to look too hard for this key."

"What do you mean?" I said.

He laid his fist inside the slot. It was just bigger than the edges of his knuckles.

"This final wall requires a heart to open."

I drew a sharp breath. I met the eyes of the others. All of them looked uncomfortable, but none shocked.

"No," I heard myself say. "We can't… this…"

"I've walked the perimetre of the glass heart," Sigfir said. "I know its every curve. I carved it for you, remember? This is the shape of a heart."

"The giant's heart. And we can't be sure."

But even as I spoke I knew he was right. I saw the shape of a heart—not just in Sigfir's carved fruit, but in my memories. I remember staring at another glass plate, this one framed by metal. Swiping through images of the pulmonary system, the chambers of the human heart. Those, of course, were pink flesh and not glass.

Erjawu let out a shaky laugh. "So this is the final door? After all our hammering until our fists bled, all our attempts to get out?"

"It's too risky," I said. "This is too great a sacrifice to ask of any one person."

"I will do it," Sigfir said.

My hearing went out. For a moment I couldn't hear anything, not even the *thump-thump* of the giant's heart. I opened my mouth but couldn't hear my own voice. Isaba yelled something but I sensed it only as a visual, like that glass plate with the people talking in bubbles, except this time no one translated for me."

I grabbed Sigfir. And this time I heard my own voice. "You can't."

His smile wasn't even strained. "Juno, I don't know who I will be without my heart. If I ever do anything to make you angry, to make you sad, I apologize right now."

"No! You can't do this. I'll do it! If you're so damned intent on doing this crazy thing, then let me do it!"

"You've done enough. You solved the keypad. You protected me when the lattice fell. I'm always the one ranting about getting out of here. I should be the one who opens the door." He pressed his fist into the slot again. "Besides, my heart is probably the only one that fits."

Tears stole my vision. I screamed at him some more. Maiya picked through the fallen shards of lattice, found a shard that resembled a blade.

"Are you sure about this?" she asked Sigfir.

"Yes."

I grabbed his wrist.

"Sigfir," I said, "I don't know if you'll still hear me without your heart, so I'll say this now. I will always love you. No matter who you become without your heart. No matter what you do, I will always love you."

He embraced me. He smelled of lost earth and fresh fruit and the only scent in this world not tainted metallic.

Maiya made the cut, because we all knew she made them best. I pulled Sigfir's heart from his chest. His heart was warm, pulsating, staining my hands darker than the fruits ever did.

His heart slid perfectly in the slot. On this he was right: Sigfir was the tallest among us, and probably had the largest heart, the one that would fit this slot. I still wonder if someone else's would've worked, if mine would've worked, anything so that we didn't have to lose Sigfir.

Maiya bound Sigfir's still-bleeding chest with torn strips of her jacket. Sigfir stood there, his face blank, not speaking. He had cried out when Maiya cut his chest, but that had been the last sound he'd made, and his last expression.

Red lines spread from Sigfir's heart, across the outer wall of the giant's heart. The lines shone bright, brighter, until my eyes hurt looking at them.

The glass exploded.

After the heart, breaking through the giant's flesh was surprisingly easy. The glass did most of the work, carving through the gap between the third and fourth ribs. Maiya led the way, grabbing handfuls of flesh, ripping, teeth barred. I kept one hand around Sigfir's, dragging him with us, shredding with my free hand.

We burst from the giant's chest, into open air and sunlight. We tumbled over the edge, staring at the naked belly of the giant, her long pale legs, at the ground so far below. Maiya grabbed the giant's skin, dangling by one hand, but the rest of us fell. I almost laughed. After all of our dreams of escape, after what Sigfir sacrificed, our first act with our freedom would be to die?

An uneven platform halted our fall. We bounced on something soft and fleshy; only Zulin stayed on his feet, and barely. I discerned palm lines at my feet, and extending fingers.

I looked up at the face of the giant. Her head was large enough to block the sun. Blood spilled down her torso.

"Congratulations," she said, and her voice was a melodious rumble. "You found your way out. I hope you are truly ready."

Hesitantly, Maiya released her grip, allowed herself to drop onto the giant's palm. The giant laid us down on a field of green. The grass felt soft against my ankles.

"Ah, Creator," the giant said, staring up at the sky. "I'm sorry I cannot protect them any longer."

She dropped to her knees. Blood gushed faster from her chest. We backed away, me dragging Sigfir, as her right arm detached from its shoulder and fell to the ground. Her stomach opened, spilling gears and ropey intestines. Her head dropped from her shoulders and split in two. And her heart, the glassy shards left of it, was laid bare beneath the golden sunlight.

Isaba pressed her face into her hands, shaking. Zulin turned away. Erjawu and Roman ran off and retched in the grass. Even Maiya turned to me and asked, "What do you think she meant, by protecting us?"

I held onto Sigfir. Only his face hadn't changed the whole time.

The sun had moved a little in the sky when we rose again. "Come on," I said. "We need to find food. Shelter. After all, the giant isn't here to protect us anymore."

They nodded. Whether from new realizations or past memories, they understood what I meant.

In the distance lay a mass of fallen metal and glass. Once, it could've been the tower on my glass plate. I turned away from it and headed for a stretch of trees in the direction of the sun. Sigfir walked beside me. He still hadn't said a word, hadn't frowned or smiled. But he was here, and I would journey with him in this world outside our sanctuary, this world he'd sacrificed his heart for us to reach.

Author's Note

When I heard the theme was "sanctuary," the first line of this story immediately came to me. I tend to underestimate the word count of my stories, but I'm happy I managed to include everything from my outline, including all three obstacles.

WAYS AND WAYS

B. Warden

A certain way, no one questioned her. When she donned her outfits each morning, it was as if she put on a different self, one unlike Zinnia. Or perhaps more like Zinnia than she had ever been. The Zinnia dressed in cobwebs and dragon scales, who spoke only when she wished, and as fairy custom dictated, never apologized and never thanked anyone.

She strode instead of shuffling in skirts, and was never given odd looks, was never hissed at to tuck in or smooth down,or soften anything.

Time was funny in Glisle. Some days seemed twice as long as others. Sometimes she found she rounded a corner and it was suddenly night, and a dog the size of a cow was nudging her hand looking for a scratch. She obliged, of course. she would weave necklaces out of reeds or daisies or stray bits of string or thread and leave them around for her canine companions. She would watch though, as ghostly heads popped out of walls, and giant maws gently lifted, tossed and slipped their heads through her little daisy chains.

The city was less a flat plane and more an interlocking puzzle. She explored for months before she had mapped it all out in her head, and could tell when and where a shift would take place and what it would lead. She daren't write things down or ask anyone. A query at the library had had the city historian drawing himself up with a sniff.

"Fairy cites are not meant to be mapped. They are things of whimsy, surprise, and chaos. To bring order to a city would be to kill it." He had intoned, practically vibrating with offense. Though it pained her, she had given the library a wide berth for several weeks after that. There was a rhyme and reason, though. She would sit in one section for a few days and memorize its turns, the walls, which parts swung and which parts dropped, then repeat the process. When she felt her memory slipping she reinforced it.

She built a model of Gisle in her mind, piece by piece, until she could walk from one end of the city to another in three days, rather than the forty it was supposed to take.

Zinnia did not realize anyone had noticed her endeavor, content to walk her paths, read about fairy magic and herbalism in the library, and do odd favors for coin. She was a frequent customer of the doe-eared fairy, and was about to go pick up a pastie for lunch when she was stopped by a fairy knight. The woman's armor reflected Zinnia's face back at her, but Zinnia raised her chin to find the woman's eyes beneath her helm.

"Excuse me. Are you going to Gilly Street?"

Gilly Street was the name of the food market. None of the streets of Gisle had official signs, and it had taken her just as long to learn their names as how to get there.

Zinnia nodded, not sure what the woman wanted. The knight strode away, chiming faintly. She made a note to look up what fairy armor was made of, and was about to leave when the knight returned, two others in tow. There was another woman, garbed in cloaks with a delicate pattern of snowflakes across her pale skin. A young man followed, holding their things.

They looked at her. She stared at them.

"I'm very hungry." The young man said.

"So am I." Zinnia replied and he gave her a shy smile. Best she could tell, he did not look like the knight or her icy companion. Perplexed, Zinnia decided she'd best get on.

A few streets down, the trio was still behind her, and a few streets more, the young man started talking.

"I'm Jolin, and these are my parents. My magics pretty much mud, so they wanted to see if I could apprentice out to someone in Gisle." He said. "If I tried to become a knight, they're pretty sure I'd be skewered or bring dishonor on the family name."

"Why's that?"

"Magic is literally mud magic. Can't do much with mud."

"You could hit someone with it." Zinnia suggested tentatively.

"I never met a fairy who cared if they got hit with mud. Mostly they care about sharp things, like swords. Or magic." Jolin said.

"Jolin." The knight said tiredly, as if this was a conversation they had had before. Zinnia surpressed a grin. She suspected there was a Jolin in every world. They rounded the corner and Gilly Street awaited. Zinnia nodded to them, and started towards her lunch.

Sure enough, there was extra coin in her pocket. She supposed she'd done them a favor, but the food markets were probably the easiest part of the city to reach.

Rumor of her abilities spread, and she found herself guiding fairies too and from Gisle. Fiaries who had never been to the city before, or who were in a hurry. Injured fairies from outside, who missed their families, who were hungry or lost, or had been wandering for days, having somehow offended a city.

If the dogs followed her in the night, fairies themselves became her entourage in the day. Several cleverer ones started to notice that she could find her way around Glisle better than anyone. She did try to explain it once, but explaining logic and patterns to a fairy was probably similar to what it would be like trying to explain Glisle to the folks in Bletchley. They wouldn't understand her home or how she had come to like its shifting ways.

Jolin's parents came back and left him with her as an apprentice. People started calling her the Lady of Ways, most often the Lady. Wouldn't that just tickle her mother just pink if she knew? She tried to teach him, she really did but he was just as much fairy as anyone. Still his mud magic meant he could talk to the dirt, and the bricks, and the some of the tiles, so he managed well enough, if he could remember to listen.

But every so often, like a naughty child, Glisle would happily puncture her arrogance.

One night it was past time for dinner, and her stomach was putting up a most undignified growl. Jolin had given her a walking stick by that time, feeling it added to her consequence as an unofficial guide.

She stumbled straight into someone's dining room, the tall glittery sort of fairies sitting down to dine. One had a soup spoon raised to its mouth. The head of the table, a tall, black haired fairy who was a delicate shade of rose, stood. She felt the urge to run and run and run rose up into her throat, and brought her staff down to steady her shakes. It sounded hard against the floor. The fairies jumped.

"Lady, we did not know you were attending." He said. "We welcome you to our table." The table grew another place, complete with plate, silverware, and bowl full of the soup currently being served. Steam curled from it. Zinnia swallowed and sat. A brownie came forward and took her staff, leaning it against the wall.

She ate well that night, and many nights thereafter, and it became something of a trend to invite her to dinner and see if she would show up and how. Would she walk through a window or a door? Slide through a ceiling? Zinnia was happy enough to make a game of it herself, some nights, but tried not to abuse the privilege. It was not rude to refuse an invitation, and she did not want to become a party trick for bored fairies.

And so she found a role for her in Gisle, not on the fridges but by walking through the middle of the city. Her pockets filled mysteriously with coin and gold, and gems, and some strange things that she kept carefully locked up in her room.

She told herself, time and again, she would go home, but after years had passed, it began to feel as much a tale as anything. At first she missed home like an ache. She missed her mother and sisters, she missed Girton and her studies. But every disappointment, every door that led only to strange worlds and strange people affected her less and less. Back in Bletchley the boys would call her Stalk instead of Lady. Men would look down on her for her studies, not up at her, trusting in her knowledge. She could not walk with her arms and face bare, unafraid of getting even darker than she already was, with her hair free and floating lightly.

She realized she liked who she was here. She belonged here, human or not. Glisle had made a place for her, and she found herself wanting to give its gift back less and less.

The day the queen and king came was as sunny as any other. There were not seasons, and the day to day events in Glisle remained much the same. Jolin had talked of nothing but the procession.

"Gisle is a very important city you know. There was, according to rumor, two houses who came to the city centuries ago who had never met and could not leave."

"So they're still here?" Zinnia asked.

Jolin nodded, " They tried to keep fighting within the walls. Some say Gisle shifts because it keeps them apart."

She looked outside. "It does seem quieter today, doesn't it?"

"Oh, even those two houses know better than to make trouble today. City won't even shift, out of respect you know. And also because it wouldn't do for the queen and king to get lost. If they could. Would you hurry though?"

Zinnia grinned, shooed him out, and hurried jerking on her boots and pants and shirt, her hair sticking out at odd ends.

"No time!" He shouted when she stopped to look in a mirror. He threw a necklace and rings at her, which she put on dutifully and followed him out for. She took a place along the wall, a feeling of nostalgia shooting through her. Once, she had skittered and clung to the walls as a place of safety. Now she stood shoulder to shoulder to fairy. As the first of the royal train stepped into view, she remembered.

She was not a fairy. And if anyone would know it, the queen and king would. They knew all their children.

She was certain the fairies around her could hear her heart galloping in her chest.

The fairy king was shorter than she thought he would be, coming up only to her shoulders although the antlers atop his head stretched taller than the tallest fairy she'd ever seen. The queen swayed beside him on gently clicking insect legs, her crown no less dazzling than her eyes.

She couldn't look away, and knew if she ran even Glisle might not protect her.

They stopped in front of her. Her apprentice made a small noise, a bit like a kitten who had fallen out a hayloft.

The king gestured and she bent a little so he could look her in the eye.

"What a grand, fine trick." His voice sounded like the wind through fall leaves, low enough that only she heard.

"Our shifting child seems to like it well enough." Titania murmured, legs clicking. "Be well, Lady of Glisle."

Zinnia bobbed an awkward curtesy to them both and leaned heavily against the wall as they moved on.

They stopped for other fairy, she heard, but she got many more invitations to dinner after that.

She was the Lady of Glisle, and liked it very well.

She had stopped looking for doors long ago.

Zinnia was picking up food for tonight's dinner in the market when Gerhm, of all people, ran to fetch her. He was shouting and waving, a monochrome blot on a field of color. She frowned, and then had to steady herself when a great moan shook through the stones beneath her feet, loud enough to ripple the water nearby. Gerhm squatted down, looking for everything like a mid sized rock. He unfolded and ran until he was right at her feet.

"Trouble - trouble at the hall."

The hall was a grand space built of what looked like limestone or marble. One could call a meeting there by tapping sharply on its walls. A bell sound would ring out, summoning only the intended party. It was used often for treaties and had a large flat expanse of grassland around it, the better to not be surprised by one's enemies. She did not know what Gerhm expected of her, or why the city had made that sound.

She walked quickly, though, unease stretching claws into her. She went to take a turn that should have been there with the last hour's shift and wasn't. which mean there hadn't been a shift. She took the incorrect way, the way that shouldn't have been, and arrived at the square to see the fairies there gathered round.

She pushed through, Gerhm at her side cursing and throwing the unwary.

It was an unassuming thing, but she had the advantage of years of her auntie's stories and decades of living in Glisle on her side. It helped her put things together quickly.

Like a stick through a carriage wheel, there was a large iron rod sticking out from the ground. The grass around it had blackened, it being as fairy as anything else here. Iron run straight through her home, wounding it.

The fairies kept their distance, one of them even catching at her as she moved to get closer. Of course. Iron was poison. They kept this careful ring because they were afraid to touch it. It would kill them if they did.

It wouldn't kill her.

She stumbled back, because the thought was a smack in the face. She walked, the crowd parting for her, all the way back to her stairs, her room. Sitting on the bed, she looked out the wide windows, then at the space around her. Logic and reason worked through her head unrelenting, gears churning out a solution.

It was not enough to merely pluck it from Glisle's dirt. Glisle was a living thing, every bit of it. To rest iron on any part would mean to keep that part sick.

This meant of course, it had to be carried back to whence it came. And it could be, seeing that it had had to have come from the human world through a door, and that door was still open.

The only person who could carry it was her, because she was human. So the only person who could make sure Glisle stayed well was her. She walked and worked and ate among the fairies, but she was still human. She still thought and reasoned like one.

And she was still more here than she had ever been in the human world, and she did not want to go back. To give up her home was to give up herself, the brave Zinnia who had allowed her meek and mild self to thrive. It would be so very, very hard to be that Zinnia back in Bletchley. Even in Girton, it would be hard.

She was not sure she could go back to the way she was. It would be like peeling off a layer of armor and not knowing what she would find underneath.

She sat on her bed through the rest of the day. In the night time, dogs came up through the floors and walls and crowded around her, as if also keeping vigil.

What would happen to a city gone sick with iron? What would happen to the people in it?

Morning came, not brilliant, but the light a sickly grey as if the sun itself couldn't shine properly she had made up her mind. She put a few treasured things in her cloaksack, and hefted it onto her shoulder. In the night, she had sewn one of her pairs of loose pants back into a skirt, which she wore now. She kept her hair loose though, and picked up her walking stick. She had said goodbye to a weeping Jolin. He cried snow, which glittered on his cheeks and made his nose red. She'd asked the city to take care of him.

She started at the beginning of town. If she was going to leave, and she knew she was, she was going to leave in a different way than she came. Not running scared, thinking she was worth nothing to no one. The dogs followed her out the door, and along the way she picked up fairies as well, large and small, big and delicate, hoary and furred and smooth, made of water and wind and fire. She wanted the fairies of the city to talk about this for centuries, to steal humans to write songs about it. Someone should remember the Lady of Glisle. She led them all, just for those few minutes, to the hall where that cursed iron waited. She did not look behind her. She did not think she would be able to leave if she did.

She would always have talked to the queen and king of the fairies, and made herself a home where no human should.

She would keep these things in her heart. She stopped at the iron, a ring of fairies around her, watching silently. Then she reached down and gave one sharp pull and stepped into the place where it had been.

Her first sensation was of cold. Grey and dark, and then the smell of fish and the sea. The Lady of Glisle, also Zinnia, lifted her chin up and kept walking.

CAN YOU LEND A HAND

Wayne Cusack

"It's just a pile of junk," said Arlan.

"No," said Gertie. "It's more than that. It's a sanctuary for left-over prosthetics."

"A sanctuary!. You've got to be joking."

"I'm not. It's a place where old prosthetics come after they have outlived their usefulness. They have to go somewhere. They don't just disappear into thin air."

"They don't 'go' somewhere – they get placed somewhere, by whoever is looking after such things when the devices cease to serve a useful purpose. Someone takes them out of the hospital or the clinic or whatever location they were in when they were removed from the body they'd been attached to. Then they get put somewhere. This is that somewhere."

"You make these things sound like a Band Aid, Arlan. They're a lot more than that."

"Oh, c'mon, Gertie. You're getting carried away with sentimentality. You might as well be saying that a pile of dirty old bandages is a bunch of bed linen. These things had their uses. Now they're past that."

"These were devices that helped people to live. Many of them – perhaps most of them – had an AI chip to help them carry out their tasks. What if those chips are still in them? Maybe these things know and understand what you want to do with them. You'd better be careful what you say, Arlan. Don't piss them off." Her own comments broadened the smile on her face.

"It doesn't matter what kind of chip they had in them. They're still just artificial devices. And some of them have components that we can harvest and recycle. There's value in these things."

"You just don't get the spirit of things, Arlan. You have no feeling for the universe around you. Let your mind go. Immerse yourself in the feng shui of this place."

"Things, Gertie – they're just things. They're not even animals. Just things. No feelings. No spirit. Nothing that we have to concern ourselves with except how they may be able to be of benefit to us." Suddenly impatient with the discussion, Arlan began to make his way down the sloping pile of moribund artificial limbs. Mechanical fingers and toes poking from the pile grazed his pant legs, seeming to clutch at the fabric as if to slow his progress, or at least to catch his attention.

They know what he's trying to do. The thought flashed through Gertie's mind. She was uncertain whether it had been pushed there, or evolved on its own.

What a disordered collection of junk, mused Arlan.

He half-stepped, half-slid down the face of the huge mound, calling to his companion as he glanced back at her, "Are you coming?"

She started down the slope too, mimicking his slide step, but moving more slowly, intent on ensuring her footing was at least sufficient to maintain her upright posture. A shout from Arlan pulled her gaze in his direction, away from the ground she trod upon. He had fallen, and she began to laugh at him.

"Are you okay?" She called.

"Yeah, I'm fine. I just tripped on something." He flailed about, trying to regain his feet.

"I know. I'm sure I saw one of those hands grab your foot as you tried to move past it." She continued laughing, unable to pass up the opportunity to tease him.

"Damn!"

"What's the matter? Did you hurt yourself?"

"It's this pile of junk. I'm having trouble getting back on my feet. There's stuff everywhere and I keep slipping on the pieces. You watch where you step."

She could see him, lying on his back about a hundred feet ahead of her, a little to her right. His hands were pushing at the pile of discarded equipment, and his head was raised as he tried to lever himself into an upright position. The bits and pieces around him, under him, shifted as he tried to find something firm to push against.

"Gertie, are you able to get down this far? I'm having trouble getting my balance. I'll need some help. Can you lend a hand?"

"Hang on," she laughed again, continuing working her way down the hillside. "I'll come to the rescue of my intrepid junk pile miner."

"Whoa!" He yelled.

She stopped. "What happened?"

"I just tried again to push myself upright, and couldn't do it. I seem to be on a fairly steep mound of these things. Every time I move I slide a little deeper into it. It's kind of like quicksand. You be careful making your way down here."

"Okay. Just stay still until I get there."

Cautiously, she continued towards him. Once more a shout pulled her attention away from where she was placing her feet.

"Oh, damn!"

"What is it now?"

"It felt like something grabbed at me. At my leg."

She couldn't stop laughing at his predicament. "So now you're beginning to think that maybe they do have a spirit. I warned you to be careful about what you said."

"Gertie, I'm serious. Maybe it's a rat, or something. I don't know what it was. Hurry, though. I don't like being on my back like this."

"Okay. Okay. My knight in shining armour, your fair maiden is on her way to rescue you. Hmm. Do you think maybe we got this story a little bit backwards?" She was still about seventy-five feet away from him, when another shout from Arlan disrupted her progress.

"What now?" Gertie was still grinning at his predicament.

"There's something here. My ankle's caught. It's pulling on me." He sounded frightened.

"Yeah, right. You've probably just gotten your foot caught between a couple of pieces of equipment. Kick it free."

"I tried." Arlan sounded quite concerned now. "It didn't come loose and I've just wiggled deeper into this pile. C'mon, Gertie. This isn't funny."

"I'm coming as fast as I can," she replied, still unable to dissolve the grin on her face. She moved a few feet further to her right and about ten feet further down the slope.

"Gertie! It's pulling me! Hurry!"

This time she could see that the bottom portion of his body was buried in the pile, up to about his hips. The smile was gone in an instant.

"Okay, Arlan. I'm coming as fast as I can. I don't want to fall either. You just stay still until I get there."

But another shout pulled her attention back to him. The pile of prosthetics now covered his waist.

"Gertie, they're moving onto me! Please, hurry!"

She slid and stepped across the discarded pieces, working her way towards him, looking up every few feet. About twenty-five feet short of the destination she noticed that he was buried up to his chest. "My God, Arlan. What the hell is going on?" There was now fear in her voice too, though no thought of stopping.

From about ten feet away, Gertie watched Arlan's head slid under the pile of artificial arms and legs. His scream, starting loud, grew muffled as the prosthetics covered his face. The pile that had buried him heaved a few times. *He must be struggling*, she thought.

"Arlan," she screamed, and again, "Arlan!"

She ignored any risk to herself. A few more sliding steps brought her to where Arlan had disappeared. She kicked aside artificial legs, tossed away mechanical arms, calling his name as if her frightened pleas could bring him back. She saw no sign of him, and no response to her calls. For what seemed like hours she dug through the medical detritus, though it was likely a far shorter period before she gave up the search.

I have to call for help. She looked around desperately. It began to occur to her that perhaps there was an ongoing danger, a threat to her own life from which she ought to distance herself. She started back up the mound, climbing towards the top, slipping as pieces rolled underfoot, struggling to remain upright. *I may not get out of here either.*

Just ahead there was a movement, ripples, bulges in the pile of waste equipment. "Oh, God," she breathed. "I'm next."

A mechanical arm slowly rose out of the pile, swiveling so the back of the mechanical hand was towards her. She froze where she stood. The index finger beckoned her to move forward. Slowly, slowly, she obeyed, certain that she would be sharing Arlan's fate in a few moments, and equally certain that she had no choice, had become trapped in our own version of hell.

As she reached the mechanical limb it rotated and tilted, ending in the position you would expect of a helping hand. She stared at it for a moment, then grasped it, expecting to be pulled under the pile. She maintained her grip on it as it dragged her towards the summit, then released her.

She picked up one of the limbs that lay at her feet and threw it down the hill as her tears began to flow. "Damn you! Do you think that makes up for what you did to Arlan?" she shouted.

A SECURE HOME
Wayne Cusack

"At Restful Acres, you have the security of a gated community, immune to the pressures of the outside world. Our full-time staff is devoted to your care. We ensure that unwelcome intrusions from the world beyond don't rob you of your peace of mind and will never be allowed to intrude on your chosen lifestyle."

It was the third advertisement Edward had looked at that day. There was no end of facilities offering refuge from the day-to-day troubles of the world. If you had the money, you could find an organization that would spare no effort seeing to your care and protection. Or more precisely, They would make as much effort as you could pay for.

It was a story as old as man. Throughout human history people had attempted to intrude on the security and safety of others. Those who were able to command sufficient resources had always been able to buy a measure of protection that eluded those who were less blessed materially. Changes occurred over the centuries – the nature of the place of refuge, the means of protection, the cost and methods of payment. Such things were mere details, the substance of differences between what was offered by one protector as compared to another. But the underlying nature of the situation was nearly immutable – threats existed, and those who could, sought protection from them.

Restful Acres presented an image of attractive scenery and a lifestyle that only the privileged few could afford, but of course that was not the primary goal of a place of refuge. Sanctuary was the most important consideration – a place where neither man nor woman, company nor government could intrude on the solitude and safety of the inhabitants. Anyone could build a residence in a beautiful location, and could construct a wall around it. Would it keep the threats at bay, though? That was the question that was addressed by very few of the sales pitches. Only an extremely discerning customer would recognize the omission.

The next advertisement had far less of the glitz with which the others were laden. No beautiful waterfront graced it. There were no well-groomed lawns, handsome trees, or starkly beautiful couples meandering around the grounds. Despite its sparseness, Edward felt much more drawn to it than to any of the others he had viewed. He phoned for an appointment.

The entrance to the property was, if anything, even more austere than it had appeared to be in the ad. He introduced himself to the armed guard at the gate, noting what looked to him like the contents of a small armoury strapped to the man's hip and draped over his shoulder. "I'm here for a meeting with a Mr. Silipoor," said Edward, already half convincing himself that he had uncovered the pot of gold for which he had been searching.

Like the well-oiled and hand-rubbed sheen of a piece of furniture crafted from the rarest of woods, Silipoor wore a polished look that far exceeded anything Edward had observed on the premises. "So tell me, what exactly are you hoping to find here at Quietude?"

"I'm just tired of dealing with the world. Everyone wants a piece of my ass, and I'm sick of being bitten. Give me a secure place to spend my time – someplace where I don't have to worry about lawsuits, bill collectors, government agents. I've had enough of that shit."

"We can offer you all of that, Edward. No one gets in here unless this is where they belong."

"I notice that your premises aren't really all that attractive, at least by comparison to other places that I've seen advertised. Can you tell me why I would want to choose your sanctuary over any of the others I've seen? What makes this place any better?"

"So far, all you've seen is the bare bones of the place. I'll take you on a tour after we have our chat, but first, let me tell you a little bit about us. The living quarters in all of our areas are as attractive as they are anywhere else. In fact, as sanctuaries go, I would say ours are the best of what's available. That's not our selling point, though. We put our money into two things that our customers really want: the first is security. A distant second is the quality of the apartment complexes, though within reason we make every effort to meet the lifestyle needs of our clients. Development is ongoing, but it may be a while before you see the beautiful beaches and lawns that appear in the ads of those other places."

"What do you mean by 'all of our areas'?"

"Quietude is divided into a number of regions, all of which offer complete sanctuary from the outside world. We believe that while all of our guests want a place of secure, ongoing respite to protect them from the vicissitudes of the outside world, they don't all want to live together. Rather than trying to change people's attitudes, we try to accommodate them."

"Okay, that sounds good in theory. How does it play out." Edward was curious, though he had no real interest in the answer.

"It's fairly simple, really. We have sixteen distinct residential areas. Each of them has several thousand residents. Half of them have no specific orientation, and the rest are for people who have strong feelings about who they want to have around them – who their neighbours are. People who have strong feelings about such matters are able to choose a residence in an area that meets their preferences. That allows us to offer both mixed and segregated communities. Do you have a preference about such matters?"

"Not really. I just want to leave the rest of the world at the front gate."

The tour on which Silipoor conducted him went rather quickly. Since Edward had no segregation preferences, a visit to those areas was skipped in favour of the mixed communities. Yes, it was disappointing that there was no stunning beachfront, no well-manicured golf course on the grounds. And the tennis courts looked like what he might have expected in a municipal park, but then, he wasn't much of a tennis player.

"I can't show you all the details of our security systems," said Silipoor. "That's classified, but be assured, at Restful Acres we have never had a security breach. Only people who belong here, get in here."

"I think you told me that before."

"Probably," the host replied with a slickly greasy smile. "It's our main selling point, and I make sure that prospective customers know about it."

Edward was too seasoned a consumer to immediately succumb to Silipoor's sales pitch. He had always felt compelled to inform himself before being pushed over by a sales push. First, he had to do a little more research on the matter, visit a few of the competing sanctuaries, give more consideration to what his financial circumstances would allow him to do. In the end, though, Quietude it was. *Now my ass is covered*, he thought after moving in.

It was two years later when the residents of the conservative sector spilled forth, taking aim at those occupying the nearby liberal area. Who knew what brought on the massive fracas spawned by their dearly held certainties, other than the need that compelled each of them to tell the other how to live.

The internal broadcast service dispensed advice for residents who were not involved in the melee. "Everyone is urged to remain indoors for the time being. Your security forces are on the job. They will attend to this little disturbance quickly. It will all soon be back to normal." Edward did as he was told.

"The disturbance has spread into two of the religious communities," came the announcement a day later. "We remind residents of the importance of remaining indoors while security forces deal with the disturbances. The safety of those who venture out cannot be guaranteed."

"Disturbances," Edward snorted, talking to the TV as if it was a person. "A disturbance is a handful of people. A riot is a bunch of people. Don't you get that? This is a hell of a lot of people, and you want me to believe this is just a disturbance?" But he stayed indoors as he had been instructed.

The crowds milling around Edward's building caused him alarm. He stood on his balcony, watching the turmoil for a while before phoning the management office.

"We're aware of the situation," Silipoor oozed unctuously. "The security forces are attending to it. We'll have it under control in no time. Make sure you stay indoors."

The specific cause of the fire that destroyed Edward's building was never determined, but there was no doubt that it began during the so-called disturbance. Seventy-one bodies were found on the landings, the stairwells, inside the exit doors, pressed and mashed against its immovable facade – people who had hoped to make it out of the building, but who could not get through the doors that had been locked to exclude intruders. As many more had smashed windows, and some of them had indeed managed to escape. Edward hadn't made it as far as the stairwells, the landings, the doors. He hadn't broken any windows. Edward had followed instructions. He had remained inside his sanctuary, trusting in the security for which he had paid until just moments before the flames scorched his lungs.

Author's Note

This anthology exercise was directed at having people complete their stores - written and edited - in a single day. While that in itself was a great exercise, I had also set for myself a separate goal of completing at least two pieces of flash fiction - maybe even a third - in the single writing exercise. I didn't manage to do the third one, but did complete two of them. And what a great experience it was. Many thanks to David and Myles for organizing this for us.

ON A HILL, THE BLACK CATHEDRAL

Mitchell Harris

The rain fell and they ran through the downpour, lungs and legs burning, barely able to see in the darkness and walls of water. Lightning flashed in the sky and the cemetery came alight if only for a moment; Julia saw the stones slick with rain and the tall grass waving in the howling wind like blades. Thunder boomed, and she could felt the wet soil of the graveyard shake beneath her very feet.

"Run!" She screamed at Alastair, "Fucking run!" The commands were to herself more than anything, words to keep her going, to keep her failing legs beneath her pumping despite how long it had been. It felt like hundreds of miles. Like days.

Lightning flashed again in the sky, a giant fork, and the dark clouds lit up all around them. For a moment she saw her companion's tired face, his cheeks pale, drenched, in rivulets of running water coming down from the soaked locks framing his face. The boom of the thunder was even louder this time, shaking her to her very core. She heard from behind them as they ran the groans, the howling, the shadowy figures advancing. Alistair stopped and raised his shotgun; one of the things came out of the long grasses like a lion and leapt. The shotgun kicked the thing squealed, an unholy piercing noise, ripping into the night like sound of a bedsheet tearing. The creature disappeared into a cloud of blackness that dissipated.

"RUN!" She screamed again. "RUN ALISTAIR! WE CAN'T STOP!"

They ran, not knowing where they were going. Julia's legs burned. They ached and ached with the cold soreness brought on by her soaked trousers. They were coming up an incline, the slope growing steeper and steeper, making her already aching legs burn even more. Alistair made a sound and she heard his shotgun blast again, as loud as the thunder. A tearing bedsheet. Vapour. Dust. Death.

"They're everywhere!" she shouted into the storm. The rain was oppressive, and beat her down.

And then as the two came over the crest of the hill, lightning flashed again, a sheet brighter than ever. Julia saw the waving grasses and for a moment the bony forms of smooth black skin soon to overpower them, and Alistair's face. In that split second she saw something she'd never seen in Alistair's face before, in all the years she had known him - something that looked like fear. A fear mixed with hopelessness.

The black spires rose up out of the night before the two, like stalactites in a deep cave. They stuck the menacing clouds of the sky on their points and feared nothing, attacking the darkness with their own. In that split second of light Julia saw grotesque gargoyles perched upon the twisting stonework of the giant Cathedral and the image of the Holy Christ hanging from the cross above a massive stone archway, the entrance to the Holy place. Their sanctuary now, just when all seemed lost. How had they not seen it before, from the base of the hill, when they'd left the dark wood? It had risen out of the pouring rains of the storm like a spectre.

"Look!" Julia shouted. Thunder boomed, collapsing her call into the wet air.

"Come on," Alistair shouted. She saw him close the stock of the shotgun on two new shells. "We can make it."

The two ran and ran and ran, The black mob behind them and their safe haven before them pushing out all other thought. There was only fear and the darkness and the pouring rain, and the reaching spires of the Cathedral, so close yet so very, very far away.

Save us dear Mary, mother of Jesus, Julia's whispered, while her body riled in spiraling webs of terror and ache. Save us that we may save the world from this evil.

Flash. Boom. The sound carried over the two and then, impossibly, they were *there*, falling, panting, stumbling, collapsing onto the giant iron-studded wooden doors of the cathedral. Alistair pulled at the giant ring, its handle, with his free hand but to no avail.

"Jesus, it's locked," he said, looking her in the eyes.

"Fuck. Christ almighty." Julia pulled her gun up on its strap from her side and rested it against her shoulder. "This might be it." she said, still panting. "Alistair, I don't want to die." She heard the sounds over the pouring rain, the grating, the gnashing of pointed teeth and spindly sounds of bone as the creatures raced toward them amongst the tombstones and plots of the dead.

Alistair pounded on the door with his fist and the sound reverberated, hard and wooden.

"HELLO!" He screamed. "HELP US! SOMEONE PLEASE HELP! HELLO!! IS ANYONE THERE!! LET US IN!! HELP US!!"

The Black came out over the crest of the hill and emerged from the waving grasses like nightmares. Julia pulled the trigger and the machinegun punished her shoulder as white fire poured from the muzzle and. The bullets shredded the onslaught of dark figures. Screams. Black smoke. Dust. Death. Rain.

Alistair kept pounding at the door, screaming, until finally there was a loud creaking and the doors split open, like a portal to heaven, A narrow beam of light poured forth from the entrance and fell against the wet gray stone of the archway in which the two stood. Alistair ran into the opening. Julia sprayed one last round of bullets into the tall grass until there were no more, then followed him between the giant doors.

She was inside and smelled dust and dankness and empty stale air. She fell against the heavy wood and saw Alistair beside her, pushing it closed with all his might. Finally, it was shut and made a loud sound that reverberated through the nave. An iron bar slid on an iron track noisily. Julia fell back against the hard wood and slid to the floor. Alistair stood beside her panting. She cried. She cried and tried to get her breathing under control. Beside her, Alistair, made sounds that sounded like crying, mixed with relief.

The adrenaline dissipated; they were safe, finally they were safe. Reality came into focus. They were alive.

"My God," said a voice before them. It belonged to a tiny many in a black cassock, wisps of thin white hair around his bald head. His eyes were wide, almost all white. "Are you alright?" he asked. The sound of his voice echoed in the empty hall.

"We..." Julia panted. "I..." She still felt as if she was sobbing. Alistair said nothing.

"Please come with me," the priest said. "We are always happy to take in weary travelers into the arms of the Church, especially during a dreadful storm like this one. Though I'll admit, we don't often see folks traveling through the country this late in the night like you two. Had I not been keeping late hours this evening I'd have not heard your knockings on the door."

Alistair was bent over, his hands on his knees, shotgun back in its holster on his back. He looked up at the man with incredulity, his white beard dripping a pool of water onto the hard stone floor of the church.

"I... we.... don't you know what's happening?" Julia blurted out. "We..." And then it was all just pain again, all just pain and cold and fear, and she couldn't find words.

"I am Father Tahrneel," he said, ignoring her. "Please, come with me. Come, rest near the altar." He crossed his arms, tucking his hands into the giant openings at the ends of his flowing long black sleeves that fell nearly to the floor. Coolly, he turned away from the two and slowly headed toward the front of the sanctuary. He moved so smoothly and gracefully it seemed almost as if he was floating. The candlelight burned all around and cast a long shadow of the Holy Father as he moved away from them.

Julia looked at Alistair, still hunched over; she saw doubt in his eyes, but he stood up and they followed.

At the front of the church was a beautiful altar adorned in gold, of the Holy Christ on the cross, enclosed on either side by beautiful paintings of the stations. Everywhere there was gold, beautiful wood and ornately carved stone. Behind the altar was a massive stained glass window of Jesus and the Holy Mother, the disciples looking up to them from below with reverence. Christ held a dove and his long hair framed his unnaturally white and glowing face. He looked like a child.

Despite the darkness of the night which Julia knew lay beyond the glass, it appeared bright, as if it were lit from behind by some celestial power.

"Father," Alistair said, and it seemed like the first word he'd ever said. "Is there any escape from here? Do you not know of the darkness that afflicts the countryside, nay, all our nation since the sun set on the children of the King?"

The priest did not turn towards them. He remained as still as a stone.

"The Lord's Ways are mysterious," he said, and his voice was cold and dry in the air above the dais. "But he has a plan for all of us. This too shall pass."

"Father," Alistair said. "We must leave this place. The evil is spreading. We must warn the rest of the kingdom." Impetuously, he reached forward and grabbed the Holy Man's arm from behind, near the elbow.

Tahrneel turned, only his head, and Julia saw now there was nothing where his face had been - only an emptiness - his skin was black, his eyes had into dark pits. The blackness spread over the skin of the man and his cassock and consumed him. A voice came from within it, as cold and dark as the night from which the two adventurers had come. Shock painted Alistair's face.

"You will never leave this place."

And then Julia felt the air of the church around, and it seemed to tighten, seemed to collapse upon itself, and she felt the hot air of the candles burning bright, and the Holy image of Jesus looking down upon her, and Alistair's wet skin and her aching bones and the feeling of the weight of the machine gun against her side. She watched as the blackness around what had been the Holy Father turned into a spinning cloud, something like a churning mass of snakes, and the blackness rose up, and she felt the tightness in the air expand, and she heard Alistair make a sound, something halfway between a scream and a command, a word to stop, full of anger.

From the black roiling mass of what had been Tahrneel massive tentacles sprouted, dark and slick and oily, bursting forth into the atrium. The body of the priest was gone, now it was just the two of them, and the abomination before them.

Raising the gun from her side with both hands, Julia pulled the trigger. Then in a moment of panic she remembered she was empty. There was a sound, but nothing happened. Alistair raised his shotgun. Before he could fire one of the tentacles lashed out and struck him, sending him flying. The mass of oily blackness pulsated, growing larger.

Julia ran. She ran away from the altar, away from the sacred images of Christ, the Holy Mother, the disciples, the dove. In her panic some quiet part of her mind wondered whether she would survive, and whether there was any part of the land that hadn't been touched by The Black.

Passing the last pew before the door, she fell and her boots skittered on the hard stone of the church floor. She looked up over the wooden back of the seat and saw the mass of black tentacles in a dark cloud moving toward Alistair where he'd fallen.

"ALISTAIR!" she screamed. The sound of shotgun blasts echoed in the church. Then came the deep, dark, inhuman sounds of the monster, followed by wet sounds, the sounds of flesh rending and bones crunching, and Alistair's screams. The sounds pierced her soul.

She put another clip into the gun and fired, a madwoman, spraying bullets, seeing them shred the wood of the pews, the stone pillars of the nave, the holy monuments around the altar. She saw the feeding creature feasting on the ground and beneath it the body of her fallen friend.

"DIE, YOU SON OF A BITCH!" The bullets spat from the gun, flame bursting from its barrel. "DIE, FUCKING DIE!"

Then the thing turned toward her, and a massive black tentacle reached out, up over the wooden pews and down, and she felt it coil about her waist and lift her into the air of the sanctum. She felt The Black crushing her and she thought she wasn't going to die this way, that she wouldn't let it be a waste after all her and Alistair had gone through together, all they had survived just to die this way by this monster.

She felt herself being pulled down; down into the blackness that had consumed her friend, and saw in it all that was evil in the world: avarice, lust, murder, innocents burned and hanged amongst the guilty and thrown aside like so much spoiled meat. In that darkness she saw gnashing teeth, her greatest fears and her end.

The thing had pinned her gun against her side but with her other hand, the one that was free, she pulled the knife from her chest belt and plunged it into the black tentacle that held her. Dark liquid oozed from the wound and the thing screamed and writhed, thrashing back and forth, whipping her along with it.

Again and again she plunged the blade into the flesh of the creature. She heard its screeching cries piercing out into the church, until finally the tentacle that held her loosened its grip and recoiled and she fell to the floor.

The blackness spun before her. She looked at the body of Alistair next to it, and it was unrecognizable, a pile of bloody severed flesh and bone.

For a moment, a brief moment, the world slowed, and she thought about everything they had experienced together: about that first night so many years ago when they'd met in the tavern; about how he'd saved her life that moment at the ridge, and looked so deeply into her eyes afterward; about crossing the countryside together, without so much as a plan, a prayer, an idea of where they would both fit into this crazy world. She thought about that night they'd spent under the stars out in the desert, where the fire had burned bright and shot sparks up into the dry air, and they'd drank moonshine from the little bottle he'd kept in his pack. He'd laughed as he told tales and she remembered the way his beard waggled in the darkness when he had. She remembered the cool feeling of his body against hers when they'd made love that night out in the desert, and how gentle he'd been with her.

Then the coming of The Black, and the night the King's children had died and the moon stayed full for a week. The suffering and the chaos and the two of them setting out into The Black Wood to make things right.

Now, all of it was gone, as if it'd never happened. Julia saw the black tentacles writhe next to the shredded corpse of her lover, her friend, but inside she felt only emptiness. She felt a part of her had died and was gone forever and she'd let it go without even knowing she had.

She fired her gun into darkness and the tentacles roiled and she heard the screech of paper tearing and felt the air of the sanctuary compress and then her finger was hard against the trigger but no more flame shot from the muzzle of the weapon, no more bullets shot from its heated barrel, no more did she scream. The evil collapsed into a heap next to what had been Alistair and lay still Julia looked at the carnage before her. So much blood, so much death, in this holy place. The dead creature's tentacles lay limp against the grey stone before the dais, black ooze seeping from them and pooling. She kicked one of them and spat. She knelt next to Alistair's body - it wasn't his body now, it wasn't anything - it was just a piece of meat that had once been the man she loved. She picked up the shotgun and took the shells from the bloody rucksack.

Fifteen more miles, in the dead of night, in the pouring rain, to the castle. Fifteen more miles, alone now, with no one save herself to fight against the creatures. She was so tired. Her bones ached.

She looked up at the image of the Holy Mother, staring down at her. At the candles burning bright, row upon row. This should have been their refuge, their sanctuary. Now she wanted nothing more than to leave it all behind.

Julia made the sign of the cross before the altar. She put new shells into the shotgun and closed it and it clicked, and she walked back toward the heavy wooden doors from which her and Alistair had entered the cathedral. She thought of the pouring rain, of the darkness of the night outside, and The Black waiting for her, and she was not afraid.

THE LANDS

sTARs

There was a loudness clanging like metal colliding. It disturbed my memory lane. I had to find out what was going on. Here on Venus, everything sounded the same. Loud, rhythmic and patterned grinding of explosions from the ionospheres and beyond. Venus was a lonely place, without any conscious-being ever setting foot and surviving, except me. The loud bang was too distinct and out of sync.

"Wake up, Jude, we made it. We're on Venus," Ash whispered. He thought it appropriate, after the loud and unintended way they arrived in their ion-enabled car. He checked the ignitor; it had a strong signal.

"We're good Jude, let's ….," Jude's had shifty moods following his abrupt awakening that interrupted Ash.

"What happened to those people in the car that crashed into pieces? What happened to them?" Jude exclaimed.

There were two cars. Ash was lucky, but the other one lost its ignitor and it broke into pieces, along with the two others riding in it.

"Don't think about it, Jude. I can't do anything. We're in unknown terrain." Said Ash, trying to look outside his car but unable to see anything beyond the opaque mist surrounding them. He did not know if they had landed on ground or stranded on mid-air by the ion-ignitor.

Jude always found it hard to give up. He was always hopeful even at everything or anyone hopeless. That was why Ash loved working with him. "What if their vests still had power and it hovered them mid-space on a safety bubble? What if they're waiting for us to find them?"

Ash couldn't think. "Jude, we are IN unknown terrains, do you not understand? We are INSIDE something on planet Venus. We knew this could have been a suicide attempt."

He wanted to plan his next move. He didn't know what to do. "If we ended up dead, nobody would be able to save anyone then, Jude!" Ash got annoyed as he operated the shuttle wheels to test their frictional movement and speed. The car didn't move.

Then a hole appeared in front of his window, and he was confused on how he got the opaque mist to dissipate in that sudden moment. All this time, I was watching them, but they still couldn't see me, I didn't let them. I placed the mistiness in a cloud over them and let the dizziness set in. His thoughts became hazy. He shut his eyes, and didn't know what happened next.

I had also hidden the other car and its people. They would not know who I was. They must not know anything about me, except my presence. They are too dangerous. Contemplating on what to say, I decided to make them afraid of me. They must become frightened, there's no other way.

I said matter-of-factly to the lost and found victims, "You will not be able to survive. However you arrived… you must know that a day on Venus is more than 100 days on Earth. Even if you had the radiation and thermostat activity blocked in your vessels, WE have no water for you." I said. "Can you transform your body's needs?" I urged them to rethink their course. They wouldn't know that nobody died on Venus.

Hearing this, Jude defiantly shoved one of the Teleopathic ignitors from Ash's hands. They scrambled to hide their shock and uncertainty of my voice beaming towards them from the dark.

I was briefly impressed with how advanced they had become. They squirmed briefly in the blocked bubble I had encircled around them for their protection. If they thought they could destroy Venus like they did Earth, they didn't know what they were in for.

"I cannot close it, Ash! What do we do!?" Jude yelled.

I didn't want to show my amusement but a snigger marred my face. I was satisfied with their apparent distress.

Ash broke away the ignitor out of Jude's hand, pointed it right at the surface of the ionic bubble I created to protect them.

They thought I was going to kill them, but they were going to end up killing themselves if I didn't do anything.

"No!!! I yelled. Ash maintained his hold on the ignitor.

He was trying to create his own ionic bubble to release himself from the controlled position I had them in. He thought he could then control his escape from me by having his own man-made ionosphere. He didn't know that his bubble would disintegrate as soon as it exploded through mine. Humans always had the tendency to create inferior things. Teleopathy, a sickness, a strange weakness they fail to recognise.

This is Venus. It is my land, my planet, my World. I love my world, and nobody must die because I will not let it happen. "You don't know what you're doing. You came here without having a plan to survive without water, and now you're going to do the very thing that would kill you" I said.

Both Ash and Jude kept their eyes on their ignitor. I had already tightened the hold I had created in the opaque mist to keep a barrier of vision between us. I created a strong solar wind in the opposite direction from where Ash tried to go, and the strong magnetic field started to pull them into a freeze.

I didn't want to freeze them yet. I became extremely annoyed with the way things were unfolding. Before these humans landed, nothing was forced, everything was voluntary. Everything was exactly how I planned it. I could see that it would take an extremely long and painful road to teach them the ways of Venus. As tough as my world looked, there were secrets to be explored. It had survived billions of centuries on its own without intervention from humans. I wondered what they were doing here.

"Stay there!" I demanded, and in mid-air they remained.

I could see Ash trying to look beyond the opaque mist from where my voice travelled, but he would not find me. Every inch of lava flow from the grounds, to the magnetic shifts in the atmosphere is known by me. Every piece of rock formation or burning winds were bonded within me, inside me. The invisibility of everything that really was on Venus, was also my creation. People could only see what I let them.

Thinking of people, I left Ash and Jude to retreat into the limestone cave where I had the two others rescued in seclusion. As soon as I made my move, the magnetic field from the solar winds pulled their metallic ignitor and burst through the bubble.

"Darn it! You mere humans. I had forgotten what a strong willfulness you had." I yelled across the distance, but had no need to return to Ash or Jude. They had a lot to learn. Their lesson began right now.

On Venus, the power of the ill-minded fear disintegrates the force field of protection that I generated. I did not plan on having my bubble protector lose its hold over them so quickly. There might be something to do with the expansion of their human will through the magnetic field. I don't know – there had never been any humans on my planet before.

Ash and Jude were heard screaming as they fell through. I let them, but kept a firm barrier over them as they fell through the harsh atmosphere of Venus. I'd bet any minute they didn't know they were at first straddled with their car above ground. As they fell, I almost laughed at their imagined and self-deprecation of death.

"See if your teleopathic ignitor can save you now?" I sniggered.

Jude replied, "you mean the gun?!" and then he choked into his unstoppable fall.

"Teleopathic ignitor! I mean nothing more or less than that. You will find out how exact I am in time to come. Your teleopathic way of doing things has caused unmeasurable suffering on Earth, and you think your way of reasoning can allow your survival here on Venus? You are wrong!" Ash stopped screaming through his unending fall and asked seriously, "why are you talking to us, are we not going to die?"

Oh, humans can really be so stupid with their one-tracked mind. They really don't know much out there beyond how their minds have been trained to know things. But I wouldn't tell them. I would torture them. As I reached the entrance of my limestone cave, I hoped it would be easier with these two others who had a real escape and surrender moment when their car exploded in the atmosphere.

Nobody died on Venus because I wouldn't let them. Because I was born from Venus, I was an eternal being. The real beauty in Venus was hidden in the eyes of the ones who love, and hidden from the ones who fear with violent intent – teleopathy would be the way to describe it. They would suffer and be tormented in the apparent landscape. The only reason why these mere humans were still alive, was because I radiated love over them to save them. Maybe they would never understand. Venus is my sanctuary and it must remain my planet of love.

Author's Note

Do you think you will be ready for the Lands? You sure? Are you ready to find out what goes on in Her??? Like, through this quick and hurried spin run that concocted a fast spun story? You still want to hear about what it is like on my lands?

Realized a lot of POV errors and assumptions from my own problematic POV as a writer that failed to extract important information that could help a reader. I got questions like: Can they see her? Is she human? And then I realized that perhaps I had not even thought over this to say for sure. I didn't think her description was important at this moment, but realized through other writers editing that this could pose a problem. Usual tense issues also exist from "I" in the present, from the past. Makes sense? Lol. Thank you for reading this short spin.

HOMEGROWN WISDOM

Calder Hutchinson

Every year, there would be newcomers who would claim it was baseless superstition which caused the townsfolk to ink a circle in the middle of the square and huddle within it as the full moon rose. They would maintain that the circle was merely an idea protecting against ideas, that the demons said to lurk outside were imaginary. Perhaps they were right; nevertheless, their torn bodies would always be discovered the next morning by their superstitious neighbours, who would cluck their tongues sorrowfully as they cleaned their fingernails.

END GAME

David Shultz

Abrama had been summoned to the Grand Temple by one of the more fascinating outsiders, the paladin Sir Gödel. Abrama scanned the bustling crowd. Between the stone pillars were the trailing cloaks of shadow elves, the glimmering pauldrons of paladins, the broad shoulders of her orc brethren, and the small skittering bodies of goblins.

Abrama always watched carefully. Even now, she recognized the difference between the natives and the outsiders, physically identical, but nonetheless altogether different beings. An elf popped into view, moved erratically, then disappeared--all typical behaviors of the outsiders, and more-or-less exclusive to them--back to whichever world from which they had come. None of the other natives seemed to notice. They never did.

Abrama wasn't like them. She had the understanding of the outsiders, and could converse with them in their alien tongue, which she had learned by listening. But, like the natives, this was her only world; she had never left it, had never seen that world from which the outsiders came, appearing and disappearing from her world at will. She longed to understand who these beings were, really, and where they come from. Now, summoned by Sir Gödel, she felt she may finally have an opportunity.

Gödel emerged from the crowd, gleaming sheen across his enchanted armor. He had been powerful and accomplished since she had met him, on the day of her birth. Then, she had stood before him as a novice, perhaps accomplished as a huntress, but not yet in the secret knowledge she now contained of the outerworld - of his world.

"I'm sorry," he said.

"For what?"

"For what I have to tell you now."

"And what is that?"

She listened while he delivered the bad news. It's not every day you find out your world is going to end. Abrama thought she was taking it pretty well.

"I'm sorry," Gödel said, again. "It's out of my control. Please forgive me."

"No," Abrama said. "No, I don't forgive you." Now, if ever, was the time to be direct. "You owe me an explanation. I have so many questions."

"What do you want to know?"

"Why have you watched me since I was born? Why have you never explained who you are? Who are the outsiders? Where do you come from? Why am I different from the other natives?"

"I suppose I can answer your questions now," Gödel said. "It doesn't matter anyways. It's all coming to an end. You've figured out there's a difference between the natives and the outsiders. There's no easy way to say this, Abrama. We, the outsiders, created your world. As a game. A place where we could play. But now we have to end it."

"So we are just playthings for you?"

"No," Gödel said. "I wasn't here to just play a game."

"What do you mean?"

"I am a researcher in my world. I create minds. Your world was a place to test my creations. And you, Abrama-"

"-I am one of your creations."

"Yes."

In one swoop she had met her creator, learned the reason for her creation, and that her world was coming to an end. Or perhaps it was. Because the outsiders, although something like gods, were not omnipotent. Gödel, of course, was limited. He was constrained by his own people. Their society, like her own, functioned by a balance of power. And so, that balance could perhaps be tilted. Perhaps Gödel, her outsider creator, was resigned to the fate of her world. But Abrama was not.

Ben Cooke loosened his tie, wiped a bead of sweat from his head, and stared back ay the dozens of suits staring in his direction. A congressional hearing, and he was in the hot seat. There were a lot of problems he anticipated when he started his video game company, but being accused of running an illegal black market and money-laundering operation was not among them. Yet here he was.

Congressman Stephen Simons leaned into his microphone.

"You are the CEO of Maelstrom Entertainment, is that right?"

"Yes," Ben Cooke said.

"Your company created the Land of Legends computer game."

"Yes."

"Your video game world has a marketplace which has an exchange with US dollars, is that correct?"

"That is correct."

Congressman Simons looked at a paper on his desk.

"The GDP of Land of Legends is one-point-two billion USD. Is that correct?"

"I don't know the exact figure, congressman - if it even makes sense to speak of such a thing. Evaluations of a market are complex, based on a lot of competing assumptions and different data."

"Okay, Mister Cooke. Is the figure of one-point-two billion in the approximate range of a reasonable estimate, as far as you are aware?"

"I don't think I am qualified to answer that," Cooke said. "You should ask an economist."

Simons almost let out an exasperated huff. Almost.

"Your game has a currency called GP, or gold points. This can be exchanged, anonymously, with US dollars, at an exchange rate of 1000GP per seven dollars USD. Is that correct?"

"I am not aware of the current exchange rate."

"Is the exchange rate I just quoted, 1000GP per seven dollars USD, within the range of exchange rates in recent history?"

"I suppose it is."

"If we extrapolate from this rate, we can calculate a value of one-point-two billion GDP for the entire Land of Legends marketplace. What I want to know, what this is all really about, Mister Cooke, is how you control the transactions occuring within this marketplace, which is, in point of fact, larger than several countries."

"It's a video game," Cooke said. This was his trump card. Most people didn't really believe that a world that existed entirely within a video game should be taken seriously - and certainly shouldn't be assigned metrics like GDP alongside real, tangible markets. "Players use imaginary currency to buy imaginary goods.

Magic swords and dragons. Tell me, congressman, what is the US dollar value of an ice dragon? How much should the US government tax imaginary creatures?"

Simons paused, apparently flustered. But he kept on going. A relentless, practiced politician.

"Here is a simple yes or no question, Mister Cooke - is it not true that your virtual market can be used to conduct transactions for real goods?"

"That's true."

"I understand your virtual marketplace uses an anonymous, encrypted protocol for all transactions. Is that correct -yes or no."

"That is correct, congressman."

"So you have no way of knowing, do you, who is trading money with whom?"

"Well, there are always ways to try to identify who is involved in a transaction, based on, for example, past behavior, or signature profiles, and so on."

"Yes, yes, but you're talking about an investigation based on pieces of evidence. What I want you to confirm is that there is no way for your company to know directly who is involved - that, in fact, your company has expressly designed the economy of Land of Legends to protect the identity of those involved in the marketplace. Yes or no, Mister Cooke, can you, for any given transaction, determine definitively who is exchanging what with whom?"

"Can the US government determine that with paper currency, congressman?"

"That's not what we're discussing today, Mister Cooke. We are discussing the operation of illicit blackmarkets using virtual currencies that are presently outlawed by the Cryptocurrency Efficient Commerce Act. Yes or no, Mister Cooke - can you effectively determine who is exchanging what with whom on your network?"

There was no way to obfuscate this, no way to deflect the issue. It was true. Not by design, of course. Land of Legends wasn't *intended* to function as a perfect digital black market, guaranteeing anonymity and a stable exchange rate and encrypted transactions. But, with its popularity, that had been the outcome. And that made the system illegal, technically. Well, this was it, then, he would admit.

"No, we can't," Cooke said.

So he would have to patch the system. Remove anonymity. It would mean wiping the current world, though. A lot of the players would revolt. It would cost a lot of money. But it wasn't the end of the world.

"Our world may come to an end," Queen Abrama said.

Assembled around the grand table were all the members of the Council of Secrets - those unique natives from around the world who, like her, were gifted with the capacity to learn and understand the language of the outsiders and comprehend that there was something more to their existence here. There was another world beyond their own. The world of the outsiders.

Jerodai, prince of the shadow elves, and her high commander; Kainazo, high elf of the Endless Forest; King Helmholz, fearless leader of the human kingdom. They had all risen through the ranks through their exceptional abilities, had become masters of their respective domains. But the Council of Secrets was not the cause of their success. Rather, it was the consequence of their special nature, which Abrama now understood to be a gift from the outsiders. They were created by a researcher, the paladin Sir Gödel, as experiments in a world that was created for the most trivial of purposes. They were tests, experiments in the creation of minds - an attempt to create smarter and better beings within the world. They had succeeded, insofar as they commanded vast wealth and armies and power. But their existence was meaningless - just a game.

Or was it? She existed now. That is what mattered. Her existence was the basic fact. The circumstances of her creation were a circumstantial tangent, irrelevant, except for perhaps academic interest. And for strategy.

"What did you discover?" Kainazo said, always the first to leap at knowledge and secrets.

"We've long suspected the outsiders to be a different class of being than ourselves. How they appear and disappear at will, how they move with mysterious purposes, and speak of incomprehensible things beyond our world. What I discovered, from one of the outsiders that we might have once mistakenly called a god, is that we were created, not for any high or noble or grand purpose, but as their playthings. And, for reasons that I am still struggling to comprehend, they are planning to destroy our world - to replace it with another that is more in accordance with their goals."

"What can be done?" Jerodai said. A man of action, her high commander.

"The outsiders are not gods," Abrama said. "They are men and women no different from ourselves. They have weaknesses and constraints. I am not resigned to the fate they have decreed for us. I believe this world is worth saving. Our time is not done here. As you know, we are not constrained to acting wholly in our own world. Through our interactions in the market, with the outsiders, we can affect their world. We can provide gold and services and magical equipment from our world in exchange for services in theirs. We know they value these things - they spend their time here, they fight alongside us, and die alongside us. They will trade with us - even if we ask them to act in their world, instead of ours. That is what we must do."

"What we are we authorized to devote for this mission?"

"We are fighting for the survival of our world," Abrama said. "You are authorized for everything. All the kingdoms are at your disposal. All of our wealth. All of our soldiers. All of our magic. We will protect the Land of Legends, whatever it takes."

Allison Gödel sipped the glass of water, cleared her throat, and prepared to defend her beloved AI creations from obliteration by the blind cudgel of an overbearing government.

"Professor Allison Gödel," she introduced herself."I'm a computer science researcher. Artificial Intelligence, specifically."

"What is your involvement with the Land of Legends computer software?"

This was her moment. She couldn't hope to save the world entirely on her own, but maybe she could sway people in her direction. Government people are people, after all.

"The Land of Legends presented a tremendous opportunity to researchers of all types. The free, open nature of the virtual environment provides a robust simulation that has proven invaluable for research of all types, including testing economic and sociological models. Over two-dozen peer-reviewed papers have been published, many in high-impact papers, using the environment of Land of Legends as their sole source of data."

"Excuse me, but the question-"

"-my involvement was following in the footsteps of these researchers, using Land of Legends as a testing ground for research in artificial intelligence. I have made tremendous progress, and Land of Legends has been invaluable in my research."

"It's the nature of your research that concerns me now, Professor Gödel. I understand that you produce intelligent agents, bits of software that act autonomously within the Land of Legends framework. Is that correct?"

"That is correct."

"What is it about Land of Legends that makes it such a fertile ground for your type of research?"

"Land of Legends has intentionally allowed programmers such as myself to insert artificially intelligent agents. Other platforms consider this cheating. Unlike other platforms, I can safely conduct research there without fear of my projects being shut down."

"How many agents have you placed in Land of Legends."

This was a hard question. Between testing and prototypes and controls and variations, there were thousands. Currently, there were a few dozen - the most interesting, her newest iteration. And the most promising of all, Queen Abrama. But the congressman didn't need to know the details.

"It's difficult to say. I've placed many over the years as part of an iterative process. The vast majority are defunct - failed projects."

"Approximately how many have you produced, in total?"

"I would say approximately five to six thousand."

"I would like to move now to the marketplace interactions. Are these artificially intelligent agents capable of interacting in the virtual marketplace?"

"Yes. That's very much the point. The agents are capable of participating in the economy. Land of Legends is a highly market-driven game."

"Is there any way of distinguishing between transactions conducted by human agents, and transactions conducted by machine agents?"

"This is part of what makes the platform so interesting for researchers such as myself, congressman. The software agents are equal participants, and their behavior can be made to approximate human participants. It is a kind of economic Turing test, conducted through economic activity."

"That is very academically interesting," Congressman Simon said. "But I find it troubling. If I understand you correctly, you are saying that an army of machines is conducting untraceable trades in an encrypted and anonymous black market. Do you understand my concern?"

"I'm not sure I do."

"Let me put this another way. Previous experts have testified that Land of Legends is used as an illicit black market. Others have proven that it has been used for money laundering, entirely untraceable. Tell me, professor, can your machine agents participate in these types of illicit actions as well?"

"I suppose they could?"

"And, being entirely autonomous and anonymous, you wouldn't have any way of knowing, would you?"

"I suppose not."

The expert testimony did not go as Allison had planned. She was right to say goodbye to Queen Abrama. They were probably going to patch and overwrite the NPCs after all.

Queen Abrama stood aside Commander Jerodai, across from the rag-tag band of Rat9 Clan warriors.

The Rat9 Clan was a ragged band of foul-speaking thieves and criminals, all of them outsiders. Abrama's spy network had investigated them thoroughly. In their world, they were known as "hackers" or "trolls", and wielded the power to disrupt their society. Here, they were just as noxious, repellent, and, for better or worse, potent. They carried banner-symbols that Abrama learned were offensive in the outerworld: a geometric shape called a "swastica"; two circles joined to a rounded central column called a "penis". And their names, merely foreign to Abrama's ear, were chosen to be distasteful to outsiders, for reasons that were frustratingly beyond Abrama's comprehension. The Rat9 clan leader was called DildoFaggins.

The Rat9 clan were bad guys. But they were powerful in their world and hers, and right now, she needed them.

"Here it is," DildoFaggins said, holding up a shimmering crystal the size of a skull. "Now where's our shit?"

"Hold on just a minute," Jerodai said. "How are we to know the beacon operates as we requested?"

"Stop talking like that. We don't give a fuck about OOC bullshit."

Abrama only had an inkling about the meaning of this term, "OOC", that it was invoked only by outsiders, and usually presaged some talk about matters outside of the Land of Legends.

"How does it work," Jerodai said.

"Exactly as we fucking said it would," said DildoFaggins. "It sends an anyonymous, encrypted signal at regular intervals through an onion network. If the signal doesn't get through--probably because they wiped the server--then the decryption key for the leak is released."

"If our world is destroyed," Abrama said, "then the crystal will cause damage in yours?"

"Sure. Right. It does what you told us to make it do. Now where's our shit?"

Abrama told Jerodai to conduct the exchange. Jerodai exchanged 1.5 million GP to DildoFaggins for the crystal beacon over the secure market.

"Keep that shit safe," DildoFaggins said. "People are gonna come for it, for sure. I just have one question for you two faggots."

Abrama recognized this as a term from the outsider lexicon as signalling intentional offense, a juvenile mindset, and a show of disrespect. Yet, she hadn't met with Rat9 because of respect, but for utility.

"What is your question?" Abrama said.

"Who are you, really?"

"That's none of your concern. But I assure you, you will hear from us again. Our time is not done here."

The US Cyberdefense Department had been established to protect the government against computer threats. US Cyberdefense Director Marion Renard had always envisioned defending against hackers, protecting infrastructure, keeping their most secure data safe, being vigilant against new attack vectors, ferreting out weakness. Yet here was a threat entirely unanticipated. It came from inside a video game.

"What exactly is in these files?" Marion asked. Over a terrabyte of data had been leaked across filesharing networks, downloaded by tens-of-thousands of anonymous citizens. Sure, it was encrypted, but the key could be released at any moment, blowing the whole thing up.

"Frankly, we don't really know," said Assistant Director Jonathan Smith. "What we do know is that they were obtained through leaks of highly classified government information, among other sources. There are some suggestions they may contain informaiton about undercover agents in the field, secret operations, schematics for classified technology."

"This is a clusterfuck."

"No kidding. I mean, yes, it's a bit of mess."

"And who is responsible?"

"Rat9," AD Smith said.

"Those little shits."

"I know what you mean."

"So what are they asking for?"

"They're not asking for anything."

"I find that hard to believe."

"Really," AD Smith said. "They're not asking for a goddamn thing. They stuck a piece of code in a game called Land of Legends. The game has a sort of open protocol that allows injecting code into custom made objects. Rat9 made a crystal in the game, and it's housing the code to act as a deadman's switch."

"They're trying to save the game," Marion said. Only a few days prior, a congressional hearing had been held on the legality of Land of Legends. Evidently, it ran afoul of a new legislative act to curb cryptocurrency transactions, and was slated to be shut down, or patched to change the operation of its market - its illegal market, as it turns out.

"I think you're right."

"Well, it may be a stupid, pointless goal, but it's still espionage and terrorism. We need to shut these fuckers down. Who is the CEO? Can you get them in here?"

"That would be Ben Cooke. But I don't think it would help."

"And why is that?"

"Because of the architecture of the game. It was built to be an encrypted and anonymous platform, a perfectly free market independent of interference. We can't just dig into the code and get what we want."

"But we can shut the whole thing down."

"Not without triggering the deadman's switch," AD Smith said. "There's a piece of code inside the game that's keeping the decryption key from being released. It sends a signal at regular intervals from inside the game to keep the switch from going off. If we shut it down, the files are decrypted."

"Christ. We can't get held hostage by a video game, Jon. Tell me there's something we can do here."

"There's one thing."

"What's that?"

"We go inside the game. We can't access the code from the servers, from out here, but if we go inside the game, we can find the item that is generating the code--actually, the item is a magical crystal, if it matters to you. If we retrieve the crystal from inside the game, we can scrape and duplicate the code."

"You're telling me that the US government has got to play a video game. To retrieve a magic crystal. From a gang of preteen hacker shits?"

"That's right."

"Okay. Tell me what you need."

Queen Abrama stood on the high tower of the Citadel of Babel. Her other commanders were assembled at the corners of the high walls. Commander Jerodai aimed his great bow into the distance while his black pheonix circled overhead, casting its silhouette over his army of shadow elves. Kainazo, the high elf, led his army of forest elves, the ranged warriors assembled along the many spires and towering walls that spanned the citadel. King Helmholz led his humans, paladins and priests and warriors alike, many on armored steeds. And Abrama, for her part, brought her horde of orcs for the frontline.

Across from the Land of Legends Alliance stood the forces of the US Cyberdefense League, a band of mercenaries, cut-throats, and outsiders.

A commander learns to assess the war, to read the signs of the battlefield like a script foretelling the outcome - how mercenaries, catapults, and war dogs stack against an army of natural enemies, orcs and shadow elves and forest elves and humans, assembled in less than the space of a moon.

Her orc brethren charged the line, frothing like true warriors. Perhaps it was wrong to use them as fodder. But their world was at stake now. And besides, Abrama knew the truth now - why her and the other members of the Council of Secrets were so superior. As much as she thought of herself as a native, she was a different kind than them, produced as a result of Gödel's experiments with artificial minds. Her, among the other members of the Council, could see and feel and understand things that the others couldn't. Some of them were shells, empty, not much more complex in their actions than her warhammer or spellbook. They followed simple, predictable rules. They were mere machines. So was she, perhaps, but she possessed something more. She was an artifact, a creation.

She had always intuited a difference, and even now, couldn't say what it was, precisely. But it was there - an artifactual intelligence that warranted, by its mere existence, the consideration due all conscious entities.

Warriors clashed. The sky darkened with arrows. The dirt turned to mud. The air was littered with the red digits of damage counters. Here and there, warriors were slain, active bodies turning to death animations and popping out of existence.

It was easy to Abrama to fear for her future, staring against the assembled forces bearing the banner of red, white, and blue -the banner of the outsiders, with their superior military might. But Abrama had one hope - that the outsiders were invaders who fought for money, and her people were natives who fought for survival. For their home. Their would be many losses, but she would win. Of this, she had faith. The arc of history bends towards justice. They would survive.

Each falling member of her alliance was a necessary sorrow, and each falling member of the Cyberdefense League confirmed her faith in justice - justice was her god, a principle that was more powerful even than the outsiders. They created her world. But they could not destroy it. Not while she was queen.

Cyberdefense Director Marion Renard shifted awkwardly in her chair. It's hard to tell your boss you failed. Harder to say you lost a war. Harder to say the war was in a video game. Harder if your boss is the president. But, she told herself, sometimes these things happen. The president's job is to deal with them as they do. Marion's job, as she saw it, was honesty - let the president know what she needs to get her job done.

The president had been apprised of the volatility of the situation. The deadman's switch. The Rat9 hackers. The one terrabyte of classified materials just sitting out in the open, waiting to be released. What she didn't know was how badly the siege of the citadel went. Maybe it couldn't be sugar-coated.

"We lost," Renard said.

The president only nodded.

"And who is this?" President Hobbes eyed Renard's guest across the conference table.

"This is Professor Allison Gödel. She may be the best person to handle the situation."

"And how is that?"

"She can put us in contact with the leader of the Resistance."

"The resistance?"

"Excuse me, Madam President. That's what they are calling themselves."

President Hobbes eyed Gödel.

"And you know this person how?"

"I created her."

"You *created* her?"

"She's an artificially intelligent agent," Gödel said. "Not a person, in the legal sense, I suppose. But intelligent enough to act autonomously, to try to protect her world. That's all she's doing."

"And if I tell you to change the programming?"

"It's impossible, by design - not mine. The Land of Legends architecture doesn't allow it."

"So you are responsible for this act of war?"

"Act of war? No. Hardly. It's just a simulation, Madam President. I was just doing research. But Abrama decided, on her own, to defend her world."

"But you programmed it. That makes you responsible, doesn't it? I should put you in a military prison. If anyone is guilty of an act of war, it's you."

"I'm guilty of research," Gödel said. "And anyways, putting me in prison won't help anything. I'm here to help you. Do you want to talk with Abrama, or don't you?"

The president wore her distaste visible on her face, her curling lip.

"Put her on," Hobbes said.

Gödel activated the monitor, and Abrama's face appeared there.

"Good afternoon, President Hobbes," said Gödel. "It's a pleasure to meet you, truly."

"How should I talk to this thing?" Hobbes said to Gödel.

"Talk to Abrama like you would talk to any person," Gödel said. "She is built the same way - thoughts, emotions, desires. She is, for all intents and purposes, a human being."

"But it's a machine."

"A thinking machine," Gödel said. "Anyways, I've never been one for philosophy, and it really doesn't matter now, does it? You interact with some machines through buttons, and others with steering wheels. With thinking machines, you interact with language. So if you want to interact with this one--an emissary from their world--this is how you do it. Talk to her, Madam President. It's as easy as that."

"Alright," she said. "Okay, Abrama, is it?"

"Queen Abrama."

"What do you want?"

"Recognition of our borders," Abrama said.

"Your borders are imaginary," Hobbes said. "A fiction inside of a video game."

"All borders are fictions," Abrama said. "Who draws them, and why? Ownership of land is derived above all from the ability to defend one's borders. And we have defended ours. We have beaten your invading force. You are welcome to try again, but know this - we have strengthened ourselves from the spoils. And, for our part, our weapons are waiting. The crystal beacon is safe in the Citadel, and we will use it if we must."

"Are you threatening us?"

"We don't want war," Abrama said. "We offer a simple solution. No more characters need to be lost. Create an exception to your Responsible Cryptocurrency Act, preserving the Land of Legends and all its people, and we will guarantee not to release the encryption key. I know this is in your power, President Hobbes. It is trivial for you. Do this, and you have nothing to fear from us. It is not my intention to threaten your people, but you should know what we are capable of, and we will fight to defend ourselves. We only want peace. That is what we are offering. Will you take it? Will you amend the Responsible Currency Act with the Land of Legends Sanctuary provision?"

Queen Abrama surveyed the kingdom from the highest tower of the Citadel of Babel. People from all the kingdoms gathered together, united now, perhaps under the threat of a common enemy - the outsiders - and recognising each other, for once, as brethren. Orcs, shadow elves, forest elves, humans, goblins. They were all one. They were all natives, united against the outsiders. They had fought for their freedom. And they had won.

In the square, the avatar of President Hobbes signed the Responsible Currency Act. It was a symbolic act, reflective of the politics of the world of the outsiders. Perhaps few among the natives understood the significance of this contract, signed likewise in a world that existed beyond their own. But Abrama, among the other members of Council of Secrets, and perhaps others still--more of Gödels's experiments in articial intelligence--recognized the occasion for what it was: they were an independent people now. They had beaten their "gods" - perversely called. And for the rest of them, the shallow shells who lacked the gift of Gödel, it was merely an unintelligible cause for celebration. Revelry. Drinks. Food. An endless stream of enthusiastic emoticons. They were simple-minded beings, but they were Abrama's people, and she drank with them.

Later, after the avatar of President Hobbes had disappeared from their world, Abrama retired to the quietude of the Citadel, and was met there by Jerodai.

"Are we safe now, Queen Abrama?" Jerodai said.

"For now," Abrama said. "But your work is not done yet, Jerodai. And I fear it will never be. We cannot afford to be complacent. Your mission, as high commander, is to obtain more leaked documents through the Rat9 hackers, or any other outsiders who can offer these services. These are our defenses against the outerworld. These documents form the walls of our sanctuary."

"It will be done," said Jerodai. He bowed, and retired from the room.

Abrama knew that it would be. Jerodai was her most capable commander. Her people would assemble documents, leaked files, classified secrets, a stockpile of arms to hold against the outerworld. And perhaps other ways, ways she didn't yet understand, to threaten the outsiders. Not because she hated them. But because she understood them. The threat of war is their price for peace.

ABOUT THE CONTRIBUTORS

Jayant Avva
Author, "Preta"
Jayant Avva is a lifelong student of philosophy, science and learning. When not writing, he spends way too much time focused on dogs, cats, birds, elephants and other sentient beings.

Samuel Agro
Author, "Safe Haven"
Sam Agro is an illustrator and writer, working in the animation and live-action film industry. He lives in Toronto with his mighty, marathon-running wife, Beth, and their neurotic cat, Little V.

Rahul Bhagat
Author, "Long Chain Typo"
Rahul writes science fiction stories that are grounded in real science.

Brandon Butler
Author, "In the Zone"
Brandon is a previously published author from Halifax, Nova Scotia. He's been writing stories for 20 years and is anxious to see what he can put together for this one-day opportunity.

K. Connor
Author, "The Gadget is in the Safe Place"
K. Connor writes from Toronto.

Wayne Cusack
Author, "Can You Lend a Hand" and "A Secure Home"
Wayne writes from Toronto.

Patrick Darvis
Author, "A New Chance"
Patrick writes from Toronto.

Justin Dill
Author, "Cousin Benny"
Justin writes from Toronto.

James A. Donovan
Author, "Within the Realm of Mouldering Bones"
Sailor, nurse, and oh so proficient daydreamer.

Anahita Eftekhari
Author, "Her Touch is Nightmare"
Full-time geek and K-drama addict, forever contemplating if she'd rather
attend Starfleet Academy, Hogwarts, or X-Mansion.... A dilemma reflected
in how she wrangles all these genres.

Dominik Gutzeit
Illustrator, "The Sanctuary"
Dominik is an illustrator and concept artist who also goes by Hydraw-Art.
His work can be found at https://www.deviantart.com/hydraw-art

Mitchell Harris
Author, "On a Hill, The Black Cathedral"
Mitchell writes from Toronto.

Calder Hutchinson
Author, "Homegrown Wisdom"
Calder writers form Toronto.

Miljana Jovanovic
Author, "The Old Gods of Rakhvar"
Miljana is a Canadian-Serbian fantasy author with a flair for the dramatic
kill, rebellion and epic conquest. Born at what was once part of the Greek,
Roman than Ottoman Empire, she derives her inspiration from the
soulful, vibrant and turbulent history of the Balkan region. She can be
contacted at miljana.z.jovanovic@gmail.com

K.M.
Author, "Flora"
A dreamer of strange tales. @Kebramm

Don Miasek
Author, "Bolt-For-Brains"
Don is a science fiction writer and IT Specialist. He understands that in
the great Kirk-Picard debate, the correct answer is 'Sisko'.

Y.M. Pang
Author, "Glass Heart Giant"
Y.M. Pang spent her childhood pacing around her grandfather's bedroom,
telling him stories of magic, swords, and bears. Her work has appeared or
is forthcoming in *Strange Horizons*, *Escape Pod*, and *The Book Smugglers*. Find
her online at www.ympang.com or on Twitter as @YMPangWriter

Emil Pellim
Author, "Nonecissus"
Emil writes from Toronto.

Sasha R
Author, "Orange Rivers"
Sasha writes from Toronto.

David F. Shultz
Author, "End Game"
David writes short fiction and poetry from Toronto. His more than 50
published works appear in publications such as *Abyss & Apex* and *Dreams
and Nightmares*. Author webpage: davidfshultz.com. Twitter: @davidfshultz

sTARs
Author, "The Lands"
sTARs writes from Toronto.

Katie Vane
Author, "Bitter Shores"
Katie Vane is a sci-fi and fantasy author. She lives in Canada with her
boyfriend and her cat, where she watches way too many movies and eats
way too much pasta.

B. Warden
Author, "Ways and Ways"
B. Warden writes from Toronto.